D1533364

What the press says about Harlequin Romances...

"...clean, wholesome fiction...always with an upbeat, happy ending."
—*San Francisco Chronicle*

"...a work of art."
—*The Globe & Mail*, Toronto

"Nothing quite like it has happened since *Gone With the Wind*..."
—*Los Angeles Times*

"...among the top ten..."
—*International Herald-Tribune*, Paris

"Women have come to trust these clean, easy-to-read love stories about contemporary people, set in exciting foreign places."
—*Best Sellers*, New York

OTHER
Harlequin Romances
by JANE ARBOR

Two Pins in a Fountain

by

JANE ARBOR

Harlequin Books

TORONTO • LONDON • NEW YORK • AMSTERDAM • SYDNEY • WINNIPEG

Original hardcover edition published in 1977
by Mills & Boon Limited

ISBN 0-373-02066-X

Harlequin edition published May 1977

Printed in U.S.A.

CHAPTER ONE

ACCORDING to the advertisement in the Paris news-paper, interviews were to be held for three hours from one o'clock, and Paula, having caught the morning Sud-Express for Bordeaux, was well with-in the deadline at a quarter to four.

She crossed the hotel foyer to the reception-desk. 'Mademoiselle Paula Raymond to see Mademoi-selle de Tourcy,' she introduced herself to the clerk who looked up and had got as far as, 'Ah yes, made-moiselle. In the writing-room, on your left——' when he was interrupted by a woman who had paused by the desk in order to search her handbag, from which she produced a powder-compact and used it as she addressed Paula directly.

'About the job?' she asked. 'Then I wish you luck, *mon amie*. But you are wasting your time.'

Paula frowned. 'Why, is the place filled?'

'Filled! Huh!' Continuing to dab powder on to an already over-matt skin, the other woman con-tinued, 'Filled? Not that I know of, nor that it's likely to be, while that one'—a jerk of the head to-wards the writing-room—'is doing the interview-ing. Doesn't know what she wants. Couldn't make up her mind to run if a bear were after her. Me, I ask myself whether, if she has two dresses, she can ever decide which one to put on. Takes your name and address, writes a bit, asks a few questions and then says, "I shall have to consult my brother". Said that to me. Said it to all the others, one hears. And I troubling to come all the way from Arcachon, if you please!'

Don't call us; we'll call you, thought Paula, half dismayed, half amused. Aloud she asked, 'Other people have applied, then? How many, do you know?'

A shrug. 'There were five before me; there may have been some who had already left.'

'But none of them, so far as you know, having been accepted?'

'Would Mademoiselle have seen the rest of us, if one of them had been?'

'M'm, no,' Paula mused. 'And anyway, as I've come all the way from Paris, I may as well see it through now, don't you think?'

'From *Paris*?' The woman's glance appraised Paula's trim short-sleeved suit and the shining cap of her gamin-cut brown hair. 'You must be more in need than you look, mademoiselle. Aren't there as good jobs in plenty in Paris?'

'Perhaps. But I rather fancied the sound of this one—as a new experience.'

The compact had been put away and the handbag slung upon a wrist, leaving two hands free for an expressive French gesture. 'Even though I tell you that the sound of this job is about all the experience of it which you are likely to get?' Waiting for no reply to this rhetorical question, Madame whatever-her-name-was turned her back and went away across the foyer and out through the entrance doors.

The clerk, looking after her, muttered the French

equivalent of 'It takes all sorts——' and turned back to Paula.

'You could go in now,' he said. 'Mademoiselle de Tourcy is alone.'

Paula knocked on the writing-room door and went in. The woman who was standing at the table, collecting loose sheets from a memo-pad and putting them in her bag, began, 'Gratien, this is hopeless! *I* am hopeless——' before looking up to see Paula.

'I am sorry,' she said. 'I thought it was my brother, who is calling for me. Who are you?'

Paula said, 'My name is Raymond. Paula Raymond. I am applying for the post as caterer-cook which you advertised, mademoiselle.'

'But after the last applicant I saw, the desk-clerk said there was no one else waiting.'

'No. I must have arrived later, though before four o'clock. From Paris,' Paula added with emphasis, in case she was to be refused a hearing on the score of her being too late to be seen.

The mention of Paris had the desired effect. 'Oh.' Mademoiselle de Tourcy hesitated. 'Oh, then— From so far? Then I suppose—Yes, I'd better take your particulars. Just a minute while I write them down.'

As, motioning Paula to a chair and sitting down herself, she rummaged through her bag for the memo-pad, Paula studied her in the light of her critic's opinion.

She might have been any age from thirty-five to ten years older. Her dress was a sleeveless, multi-coloured sack and incredibly she wore her hair, which had some attractive reddish lights, in the decades-old fashion of plaited 'earphones' at each side of her head. Her eyes were a light, vague blue beneath fair unpencilled brows, her complexion, innocent of make-up, had the papery quality of a skin which would wrinkle early. But her hands, of which the fingers were riffling fruitlessly through her bag, were lovely, Paula noticed.

At last Paula sat forward, indicating the memopad which was still on the table. 'Was this what you were looking for?' she asked.

'Oh. Oh yes. I thought I had put it away.' At least there was a ballpoint handy and Paula's name and address were duly noted in writing. Then Mademoiselle de Tourcy achieved a direct question.

'From your accent I don't think you are French, are you?' she said.

'No. I'm English,' Paula told her.

'Oh. Oh dear. That is, you speak French very well, but that is a difficulty——'

'Need it be?' Paula urged. 'I have been training and working in France for nearly four years—in catering, and teaching dietetics and cookery, and I'm pretty fluent, wouldn't you say?'

'Yes, indeed. But with our special needs at the château—That is, I do rather doubt whether, being English, you could—Or that my brother Gratien would consider——'

So this was it, thought Paula. Madame-in-the-foyer had been right. At any minute now she was going to be thrown out on the 'I must consult my brother' note, and it wasn't fair. She had the qualifications and experience. She wanted the job without needing it, which was quite a different thing, and she was pretty confident she could tackle it, given the chance. Deciding a firm line must be taken by somebody, she said,

'From the little your advertisment told me, I thought I did understand what you are looking for, mademoiselle. It said—A resident caterer and supervisory cook for the period of the vintage only, when the Château de Tourcy entertains guests and clients at each weekend. It mentioned a salary which I thought good, and as I felt I might qualify, I applied. And I didn't suppose, other things being equal, that my being English would hamper my chances at all.' In order to press home her point she produced her small sheaf of references and handed them across the table. 'My testimonials, mademoiselle.'

Her companion snatched at them as if at a lifeline. She read them through and looked up. 'Yes, well, these are excellent,' she allowed. 'You hold a Cordon Bleu, you have done luncheon and dinner catering in England, you have taken a course with Napoule le Tyr and you have taught your subject in a finishing-school.' She paused, still scanning Paula's papers as if she expected them to suggest what should be said next, when the door opened and a man, presumably 'my brother', came in.

He was tall, a darker edition of his sister as to hair, which was a true russet, eyes and skin. But the soft lines of her face had no parallel in his lean, hard jaw, firm-cut mouth and long chiselled nose. And when he spoke his voice had none of the hesitant, die-away quality of hers.

9

He glanced briefly at Paula. 'You have not finished?' he asked his sister.

'No. That is, I thought I had. But Mademoiselle here—Mademoiselle Raymond had come down from Paris, and as I hadn't engaged any of the others, I——'

'You haven't found anyone suitable—from how many?'

'Er—eight, I think, before Mademoiselle. Or perhaps one should say Miss Raymond, as she is English.'

'*English?*' His emphasis made almost an accusation of the word, and Paula flushed as his sister belatedly introduced him to her. 'My brother, Gratien de Tourcy,' she said, and then to him, 'Yes, but she has good credentials. I have read them, and——'

As he put out a hand for Paula's papers he studied her with cool appraisal. Determined not to appear embarrassed, she held his glance until he began to read. His sister ventured, 'You see, she has a diploma from le Tyr,' but he made no comment until he flicked the last sheet with the back of a forefinger. 'And this is the latest reference you have?'

'Which is that?'

He turned it towards her and after a moment's pause she nodded. 'From the Mesdames Varron, yes. They were the widows of two brothers, and I only left because they were giving up their finishing-school last Easter.'

'Where you had been teaching for close on two years.' When the next question he might have asked did not come, she felt relief. He squared off the papers and handed them back to her. 'You know,' he said, 'with such permanencies behind you, I'm surprised at your considering a short-term post like ours. Are you sure you aren't seeing it in the romantic light of a near-vacation in a wine-region château?'

'Of course I'm not,' she retorted. 'And I'm surprised, monsieur, that you think I'd trouble to do the double journey in one day between Paris and Bordeaux, simply for the chance of a paid holiday. When I happen to want one, I can choose my time for it, and pay for my own.'

She heard his sister's sharp-drawn breath, but he appeared unmoved by the dudgeon he had provoked. 'I merely asked,' he said. 'Before we advertised as far afield as Paris we probed the local talent, one specimen of which made no secret of her belief that she was on to an easy thing, while another left us with the impression that her interest was mainly matrimonial—namely, that during her stay with us she had hopes of making a conquest from among our wealthy and eligible guests. Isn't that so, Louise?' he appealed to his sister who, though she nodded, added the faint protest of, 'But, Gratien, you insult Mademoiselle.'

'As she has already made clear,' he agreed urbanely. 'And so, what did attract you to applying for the job, Miss Raymond? May we know?'

With an effort Paula answered him levelly. 'I saw it as a new experience,' she said. 'In my own line, but different. An aspect of it which I hadn't tried before.'

'Except, surely, in your freelancing days, when you were arranging public meals and functions?'

11

'That was in England,' she pointed out. 'Where I was familiar with all the available food, and almost always knew what would be popular and accepted. I was also dealing with English staff. Whereas in France——'

'In other words, you saw the Château de Tourcy as your guinea-pig for experimenting in our national foods and trying your expertise with French staffs?'

'Not at all,' Paula denied hotly. 'I've dealt with French food. I've managed French kitchen staff. The difference would be in doing it in a private house —a great private house, like a château.'

'And the prospect doesn't daunt you at all?'

'I saw it as being rather exciting.'

'Also as ultimately providing another testimonial for your quiver?'

She nodded gravely. 'If I gave satisfaction, I'd hope so.'

He turned to his sister. 'Seems we have here a career woman, Louise,' he said. 'Worth briefing her on the details, would you say? Or have you done so already?'

'No. I hadn't time.'

'Yes, well——' he had turned back to Paula. 'If by a "great house" you are thinking in terms of, say, Chenonceaux or Amboise, you will be disappointed. De Tourcy is no palace; it's a roomy family house on the Dordogne between Libourne and St. Emilion—the red wine country, where we crop about thirty hectares of vines, largely for red wines, though we market some whites too. In the region, the peak period of our year is the six weeks or two

12

months of the vintage, when we entertain almost continually—friends, valued business clients, prospective new ones, connoisseurs, journalists and wine-columnists from all over. Not all at once, of course. They come and go, mostly at weekends, though my late mother's goddaughter and her brother will be with us as house-guests for the whole time. If you come to us, you would have your own quarters, a miniature suite in one wing, and you would live with us as family when we are alone, but for these two.'

'And the kitchen staff?' questioned Paula.

'Our own permanent cook, her two helpers, a boy and a girl, and a scullery-lad. Do you drive a car?'

'I haven't one, but I have a valid licence, and I can.'

'Then there's a small one you can use for marketing in Libourne or St Emilion, whichever you choose. We would arrange dates by letter. Do you regard the salary we mentioned as satisfactory?'

'Quite, I think. Do I take it then that you are offering me the post, monsieur?'

'If I am, do I take it you are accepting it?' he countered.

'As long as the fact of my being English isn't going to act as a millstone of prejudice round my neck—yes,' she retorted with spirit.

He stared, then laughed shortly. 'Congratulations on a turn of repartee that would do you credit in your own language, let alone in ours!' he said. 'And you should forgive us our natural bias against English cooks. After all, as a nation you haven't the highest reputation in the matter of *haute cuisine,* have you?'

'No? Yet I've had meals in some three-star French restaurants which would disgrace a roadside canteen in England!'

'Then it's up to you to prove that the English can do better, isn't it?' he said unanswerably, then addressed his sister again. 'I think we may decide to engage Miss Raymond, Louise. What do you say?'

'I? Oh yes. Yes—I think so. That is, if you do—really?' she answered.

His dark eyes, turned on Paula, were provocative. *'Faute d'une française,* I do think so,' he said, then offered her his hand in such obvious dismissal that she had to take it, before giving her own to Mademoiselle de Tourcy and murmuring a conventional parting to them both.

Faute d'une française indeed! For want of a Frenchwoman! The nerve of the man to say it to her face! If he had intended to rouse her to further retort, why hadn't he given her time to make it? Or if his comment had been a genuine criticism of her shortcomings, why not voice it in private to his sister, and act on his doubts by turning her down?

Instead, in the same breath he had confirmed a choice which nobody had forced him to make. Certainly *she* hadn't been twisting his arm to offer her the job. But since he had—*since he had*—the Château de Tourcy was going to learn what an English cook could do!

Ten days later her train was again nearing Bordeaux, where she was to be met and driven the forty kilometres to the Château.

She had taken the train luncheon an hour earlier, lingering over it. Now she was sorting through her handbag, tidying it and putting her ticket ready for giving up. In a zipped compartment of her bag were her testimonials, and she looked through them idly.

There was her Cordon Bleu diploma; some enthusiastic eulogies from English firms for which she had arranged business luncheons during the year she had worked freelance; her passing-out diploma from the great Napoule le Tyr's School of Gastronomy, and the testimonial from the Mesdames Varron, which Gratien de Tourcy had questioned as being the latest reference she had.

She fingered it now, her honesty querying whether, in answering him as she had, she had been guilty of a lie by omission. Or, since he hadn't asked how she had occupied her professional time between Easter and late August, had she been entitled to withhold the information? She remembered she had paused, wondering, and then had decided against a candour for which she hadn't been asked. Her conscience clear, she decided the same way now. The Varron reference *was* the most recent she had to show, and the unsavoury happenings of the summer months had left no mark on her reputation except in the accusations of people whose judgement she could afford to discount.

Madame Annick Sallust. Her husband, Antoine Sallust. Their large grey house and grounds at Barbizon which housed Madame's exclusive finishing-

15

school for the daughters of the élite, and which Paula hoped she would soon forget as the scene of the most humiliating experience of her life.

There was no obligation upon her to recall it for the information of anyone else. Blot it out. Forget it. It had no significance now.

The great train had reached the suburbs of the city; the drag of brakes leashed its power and it slowed for entry to the station. People began to jostle, collecting their belongings. Paula gathered hers, stepped down upon the platform and followed the crowd to the exit gate. But before she reached it Gratien de Tourcy approached her. He greeted her, took her valise from her and turned to walk beside her.

'You had a good journey?'

'Very good, thank you.' They were as polite and formal as if they hadn't last parted on his oblique note of criticism.

From the platform he branched off across the concourse, taking her to his parked Mercedes, where he put her into the passenger seat and stowed her luggage.

'I have to collect two other passengers,' he said. 'Our young friends who are coming up from Cannes, and whose train time happens almost to have coincided with yours.'

He went back into the station and Paula waited, watching the busy city to-and-fro which she always found exciting. She watched a long taxi queue diminish at its head, without ever shortening at its tail. She followed the progress of a family of eight, all of them, except for two dogs on strings, pack-laden according to size, and returning, she supposed from some happy camping-ground, to judge by their boot-polish tans.

There were the newspaper kiosks which were being mobbed for the Paris journals which her own train had probably brought down. There were fruit stalls piled high with the seasonal peaches and grapes of the south. There was a skinny cat (why were French cats always so narrow?) threading its safe way among all the treading feet. There was——

But her general survey ended as she noticed Gratien returning, accompanied by two late teen-agers, both clad in the faded jeans and shirts of the current fashion. The girl was animatedly claiming Gratien's attention; but the boy looked about him with no more than bored interest. Paula judged him to be a little older than his sister—probably nine-teen or twenty. The girl—but wasn't there some-thing familiar about the girl? Or was it that, dressed as she was and with her long straight hair, she was merely the replica of a dozen other girls of her age?

And yet, as they neared the car, Paula realised with a chill recoil that she did know her. Not the boy, whom she had never seen before, but the girl was—— And what was more, the recognition was mutual and instantaneous on the girl's part as she stared at Paula, open-mouthed with surprise.

Gratien made their introductions to Paula. 'Monique Gautier. Milon Gautier—Miss Ray-mond,' and Paula, nonplussed but resigned to the unlucky chance, was about to say that she already knew Monique, when she caught the girl's wide-eyed look of alarm, compelling Paula to understand the almost imperceptible shake of her head. Monique didn't want to be recognised; didn't mean to admit she knew Paula. Look, head movement and her limp handshake said it all; she was as much a stranger to Paula as was her brother; the summer they had shared at Barbizon did not exist.

She and Milon got into the back seat. Monique, her poise regained, sat forward with crossed arms on the curve of Paula's seat and talked to Gratien.

'You are a *type*!' she accused him. 'When you said you were escorting your new cook to the château, and I asked if she was fair, fat and forty, why did you let me think she was?'

'Did I? Perhaps because I believe in leaving people to their own first impressions,' he offered carelessly. 'Or perhaps with the idea of giving the children a surprise.'

'Children!' she pouted. 'Gratien, I'm eighteen!'

'You were still surprised when I introduced Miss Raymond.'

'But of course I was, as you saw.' Paula had to admire the adroit way in which Monique used the loophole he had unwittingly given her, as she went on, 'I mean, she is not even fair—she is brunette and slim and young, and I bet you didn't think I'd dare tell her what you said about her.'

'As I remember, I said nothing which described Miss Raymond,' he corrected. 'And now, if you don't mind, Monique, you will stop discussing her as if she weren't listening, and allow me to concentrate on the traffic.'

At that Monique sat back, but continued to make

conversation with Paula as if they were indeed meeting for the first time.

How long had Paula been working in France? Was this her first experience of catering for vintage-season parties? She, Monique, had never been to England. Paula must tell her what to see when she went. She was free, now that she had left finishing-school.

Milon, who had the air of being a student, but didn't mention his university, confined himself to answering Gratien's occasional questions about their mother, saying she was still in Cannes, though thinking of moving to Antibes for the winter; agreeing with Gratien that she never stayed for very long anywhere, claiming she needed new scenes and shops and new people to know.

Beyond the outskirts of the city the country opened out and the commercialism of the great Gironde estuary gave place to neat vineyards, distant wooded hills, and walled estates and glimpses of mansions, in contrast to the wayside huddle of villages where vines climbed and rioted over every cottage door. Within a few kilometres of the château they came upon the Dordogne, flowing with a lazy blue glitter, seemingly denying the long range of its journey from the high gorges of its source.

The de Tourcy estate was not walled, the château itself being almost nakedly exposed to its own vineyards, separated from the nearest of them by wide driveways and square lawns, but no bordering hedges. Above the upper windows its walls were crenellated, and its red pantiled roofline was a series of *pigeonniers*, the conical towers like witches' hats, which were, Gratien told Paula, the architectural signature of the region.

The door was opened by a maid, who took in the bags as Gratien unloaded them, and stood waiting for his instructions.

'Mademoiselle Louise?' he asked her.

'She is resting, monsieur.'

'Then don't disturb her. Take our visitors to their rooms. Milon, help Berthe with the bags, will you? We'll meet before dinner for a drink.'

Paula's quarters were at the extreme west of the house on a transept corridor, a tiny suite of bed-sitting room and bathroom, originally converted, she judged, from a bedroom and adjoining dressing-room. There was a small balcony to the main room, and the windows of both looked out over a formal garden and beyond to a spread of golden bracken beneath tall straight-boled trees.

Berthe the maid surveyed the appointments of both rooms with a careful eye, murmured, 'Mademoiselle will content herself here?' and left, giving Paula her first undisturbed chance to ponder the mystery of Monique's behaviour. There had to be an explanation, and Paula's intuition told her it wouldn't be a trivial one. If she read fear aright, there had been fear of something in Monique's eyes. But of what?

She hadn't to speculate for long. As she had half expected, she had barely begun to set out the personal things she had taken from her case, when there were hurrying footsteps on the parquet of the corridor and Monique plunged into the room without waiting for her knock to be answered.

She was panting a little. 'I asked Berthe where they had put you,' she said. 'We're right at the other side of the house; two of the guest-rooms—— But look, I had to see you as soon as I could. Because I don't understand. Why don't they know?'

Paula couldn't pretend she didn't understand the question. 'That we were both at the Sallusts' during the summer term, you mean?'

'Of course. Why hadn't you told them that you were there?'

'Because neither Mademoiselle de Tourcy nor her brother asked me.'

'But when you go for a new job, aren't you expected to tell what you've done before?'

Paula nodded. 'Yes. But I hadn't a testimonial from the Sallusts, and as they didn't question where I had been since I left the Vincennes school at Easter, I didn't mention Barbizon.'

'Oh——' Monique was dark and olive-skinned, of the French type known as *jolie-laide*, neither pretty nor plain but expressive, and as she pulled at a lock of her hair and tucked it beneath her ear, her calculating stare at Paula was distinctly ugly.

'Oh,' she said again. 'I see. Or I begin to. You didn't mention Barbizon because you didn't want to admit that you'd been sacked for——'

'I resigned,' Paula corrected.

'You *had* to resign.'

'I chose to. The Sallusts had nothing against me.'

'Nothing they could prove about Madame's brooch, no. She got it back. But the rest—about Antoine in the *pavillon*. They said you were almost

21

caught, and Antoine admitted to Madame that you had been meeting there.'

Paula said coldly, 'Monsieur Sallust lied. I never met him secretly in that summerhouse or anywhere else. I couldn't stand the sight of him. He made my flesh creep. And all I knew about the brooch was what we all knew—that it disappeared from Madame Sallust's jewel-case and was later found on the corridor outside my door. The idea being that after her husband had made me a gift of it, he had got scared and had asked me to "lose" it somewhere where it was sure to be found. Which it was. Though as if, supposing I had been guilty of accepting it from him, I'd have "lost" it just there! But as it tied in with his story of our *pavillon* meetings, Madame decided it all added up.'

'Why didn't you deny it all?'

'Do you suppose I didn't? But Madame had to find a scapegoat; she couldn't have been married to Antoine Sallust as long as she had been without knowing the kind of wolf he was. *Someone* had been in the *pavillon* with him, so what more likely than that the same someone had been given her diamond drop-brooch before it turned up again near my room? And as Antoine had implicated me in the other affair, she thought that was evidence enough.'

'You could have sued her for—for something of character,' Monique was lost for the word she wanted.

Paula supplied it. 'Defamation. Yes. But I despised them both so much, I wouldn't stoop to it. I resigned, and so far as I was concerned, the thing finished there.' She paused, as calculatingly alert as

Monique had appeared earlier. 'What I don't under-stand,' she said slowly, 'is why *you* didn't want to acknowledge me in front of Monsieur de Tourcy. We both recognised each other, but you signalled silence to me, not I to you. Why was that?'

Monique did not answer at once. She crossed to the window and toyed with the blind-cord. 'I thought that if you hadn't told them already, it was because you didn't want them told about Barbi-zon, so I signalled to you that I understood.'

Paula said, 'No. As soon as I saw you I was quite resigned to your recognising me. I had nothing of importance to hide. But you—— You looked fright-ened, and I believe you still are. Why?'

There were minutes of silence. Then Monique uttered one word: 'Think.'

Paula thought. 'I can't——' she began, then stop-ped as a repellent possibility dawned upon her. She said slowly, 'You're not telling me, surely, that it was you who had been meeting Antoine Sallust in the garden? Oh, Monique, *no*!'

Monique addressed the window. 'Several times,' she said. 'That last time we were unlucky or fool-hardy. We had met too early; it wasn't dark enough, and the only luck we had was that I got away with-out being identified, and Antoine held his tongue.'

'Until he lied, and named me.'

'Yes. I didn't want that. But he didn't consult me. And I dared not tell Madame the truth. I'd have been expelled.'

Paula protested, 'But Monsieur Sallust was a married man! And nearly middle-aged—at least forty. You must have been mad to get involved with him in the first place.'

'Not mad. Just bored. And he was a man, wasn't he? Finishing-school indeed—a nunnery, more like! Just a bunch of females cooped together for weeks on end, and Antoine the only male in sight. There was the brooch too. He was in love with me, he said, and he wanted to give me a valuable present. I thought he had bought it and I was thrilled. But he told me later that Madame kept him short of money, so he had taken it from her jewel-case, and then panicked and asked me to lose it somewhere where it was sure to be found. So I did,' Monique concluded the ugly story.

Paula drew a long breath. 'I see. So Madame wasn't the only one to do some adding up. You laid it on so cleverly that she could hardly help herself.'

'I didn't do anything until Antoine had involved you, and it was his idea to put the brooch outside your bedroom door,' Monique claimed.

'And now?' Paula invited.

'Now what?'

'Well, is it a case now of thieves having fallen out, or are you still infatuated with the man? Have you been seeing him since?'

'Seeing him? How could I? I've been down on the Riviera since I left Barbizon at the end of the term. It's all over, finished.'

'So thank goodness for that. Meanwhile, who does know about it? Does your mother?'

Monique spun round. '*Mon dieu,* no!'

'Your brother?'

'No. No one does.'

'It's all behind you, in fact,' Paula suggested. 'But if it is, and you can leave it there as a silly flirtation with some nasty overtones, why were you so frightened at the sight of me?'

'If I showed it, it was because I didn't know how much you knew or guessed. And when I realised you hadn't told Gratien or Louise anything, I had to warn you that you mustn't—at all costs. Because it wasn't just a flirtation. Antoine was too experienced to let it stay that way. And I daren't—daren't, I tell you—risk my mother's or Gratien's learning that I'd had an affair with a married man.'

Paula sighed. 'Mothers forgive daughters, you know. And if it's true that it's all over now, would it matter so much if she knew?'

Monique shook her head. 'She mustn't. She, least of all—— Or no, that's wrong. Gratien, least of anybody. Maman would be angry and call me a fool, but Gratien would never forgive me. And—I've got to marry Gratien, you see,' she finished in a flat matter-of-fact tone, as if she were stating a truth which Paula already knew or expected to hear.

CHAPTER TWO

PAULA, astonished and aware of an inexplicable stab of shock, echoed, 'Got to? What do you mean?'

'Just that,' Monique confirmed in the same flat voice. 'That's why I'm here; why Maman sent me. And I have so little time—just six weeks for getting him interested and to the point of asking me. If he did, Maman would settle for that, because she knows he wouldn't back down afterwards. But if he had a suspicion of any scandal about me, he wouldn't ask me. The de Tourcys are like that'—there was a cynical curl to her lips—'they trace themselves back to the Middle Ages and beyond, and Gratien would as soon think of marrying damaged goods as he would——'

Bewildered protests jostled for utterance in Paula's brain. 'But you can't just arrange things like that—in cold blood!' she said.

'Maman can, and does. She has to.'

'Why has she?'

'For the money. We haven't any.'

'But you live in the most expensive region of France, and you went to finishing-school!'

'Madame de Tourcy, my godmother, left some money in trust for that, and Maman says she can't stand the climate further north. But it's not true that she moves about for change of scene as Milon told Gratien; it's because she is always trying to catch up on debts, and she has to look for cheaper places to live until she clears some of them off and can start again.'

'You haven't a father?'

'No. He is dead. He left some money, which should have been enough. But Maman loves clothes and parties and people, and then there's Milon too.'

'What about him?'

'He wanted to go to the university at Lyon. But he didn't make the grade in exams, and now he is drifting, doing nothing and living on Maman. As I am too until I—— Anyway, that's why I must marry Gratien if I can. He is rich and we are poor. It's as simple as that,' Monique concluded with a raw candour which made Paula's blood run cold.

'And you are eighteen, and he is——?'

'Thirty-two. It's not such a big difference, that way round.'

Between a man and a girl it wasn't, as Paula knew well, and couldn't explain her fierce longing to disagree. She said, 'But love—doesn't that come into it at all? Do you love him, or has he shown signs of being in love with you?'

Monique said slowly, 'I could love him, I think. He is rather glacial and king-of-the-castle, but he is attractive, and as for his falling for me, I've just got to make him aware of me as a woman, not a child. I must; I owe it to Maman, to her peace of mind.'

'And to her ambitions. And if you are really concerned for her peace of mind, I should think you could do a lot for it by getting yourself a paid job,' suggested Paula.

Monique pulled a face. 'Oh, don't lecture me,'

she said. 'You're not in the classroom now, and I don't have to listen. Besides, what did I ever learn at finishing-school that would fit me for a job?'

'I wouldn't know. I didn't go to one myself.' Returning to her unpacking, Paula added, 'I'm glad you've told me what all the secrecy was about. But I don't think you can expect me to sympathise.'

'I'm not asking for your sympathy, only for your co-operation. You've got to go on pretending we never met until today. Because if you don't——'

Paula straightened. 'If I don't? You mean we're both going to look rather silly, if we admit to knowing each other, when we didn't say so at first sight?'

'More than silly,' Monique corrected. 'If you let anyone here suspect that you know all this about me, you're going to be sorry. Very sorry indeed. Because I shall deny every word of it. I shall tell them that I kept silent for your sake; that you asked me to, because you had been sacked for suspected theft from the Sallusts', and as you've admitted you haven't mentioned your being at Barbizon, whose word do you suppose they will take—yours or mine?'

Paula turned back to her task. 'Oh, go away,' she said wearily. 'You've been watching too many TV thrillers about blackmail—pistols pointed at heads and hideous dooms threatened——'

'And if you don't believe that blackmail works and the dooms can happen to people, then I'd say you haven't learnt anything from whatever thrillers *you* may have watched!' was Monique's parting shot, before she flounced out, though pausing at the door, holding it open for Louise de Tourcy, who was on the threshold.

'Monique, *chérie*!' They kissed each other's cheeks. 'I'm sorry I didn't welcome you when you arrived. But I had warning of a migraine—you know I do suffer from them—which, happily, hasn't developed. And Milon, he is well? And Miss Raymond?'—she went to give her hand to Paula—'you had a good journey, one hopes?'

'Very good,' said Paula. Monique said she was going to shower and change, and Louise told Paula, 'I am glad that you two are making friends,' adding, 'I wondered if you might like to see the kitchens and meet the people you'll have under you, before dinner?'

Paula agreed that she would, and was to find her working quarters all that she could wish. The main kitchen was huge, its ancient granite walls and its ceiling a series of thick stone arches, in strange contrast to the modernity of its appointments—streamlined fitments, shining working surfaces and up-to-date ovens and grills. Beyond were the sculleries, equipped with stainless steel, and beyond the spacious larders and a cool, stone-flagged dairy, giving on to a shady courtyard and a sun-drenched drying-ground.

Louise left Paula to explore, while, explaining that this was their rest-time, she went herself to round up Paula's colleagues-to-be. Meeting them, prepared for the same prejudice as she had incurred at the hands of their master, Paula was a little apprehensive of her reception. But to her relief she seemed to be regarded with curiosity, rather than the hostility she feared. In fact Emilie, the household cook, seemed to take pride in introducing

Paula to her underlings as if she were her own invention.

'Look then,' she adjured Rosalie and Pierre, her teenage assistants, 'Mademoiselle is English—imagine that! Now we shall learn some new ways and dishes, and she will learn some of ours.' At which Rosalie executed a surprisingly old-fashioned bob of welcome, and Pierre offered the grip of a strong brown hand.

'Do they all live in?' Paula asked Louise on their way back through the house.

'No, none of them,' Louise told her. 'Nor Berthe, our parlourmaid. We also have daily women to clean, but they all prefer to live out, in their own homes in the village, going to and fro on their bicycles. It is very different from my mother's time, when we kept a staff of a dozen or more, all of them resident. But it is the same all over France now. Isn't it also in England?'

'Indeed it is,' Paula agreed. 'People who always kept several maids now make do with a daily helper. Did you lose your mother very long ago, mademoiselle?'

'No, less than three years ago. My father died four years before her, and Gratien has managed the estate since then. Maman was a wonderful hostess; even as a widow she gathered people about her and entertained lavishly all the time, not only for the vintage season. But I'—Louise spread her hands emptily—'have none of her genius. Gratien takes after her; he has far more flair than I for demanding and drawing out the best of people. He expects it of them, and somehow they don't disappoint him. The first two vintages after Maman's death were disasters. I tried to organise the first myself, and Gratien, knowing how I had suffered over it, arranged for our next year's entertaining to be done in public restaurants. But that wasn't a success either; Gratien needs a private table and hospitality for his professional business with clients. And so, although the wines we produce are only classed as "*petits châteaux*" he decided this year to entertain here as we used to in Maman's day, and to call in skilled help for the catering and the supervision of the cooking service, as do many of the châteaux with more famous names than ours.'

'Who sees to the domestic arrangements for your guests—those of them whom you have to stay?' asked Paula.

'Berthe and I can manage that, with the help of the daily women. Naturally Gratien chooses the people he wants invited, and he sends out invitations. I do the flowers myself, for that is work I love —one of the very few things I do well.'

Paula smiled. 'You're too modest, mademoiselle. Are you artistic in other ways too?'

'Oh'—another limp gesture of the hand—'I try to sketch a little, to paint. I have turned a small room next to mine into what I call my studio, but I have only very small talent, I'm afraid.'

'Had you ever thought of giving it your full time —of training at an art-school, perhaps?' questioned Paula.

Louise sighed. 'Often—when I was younger. But Papa disapproved of careers for girls, and as I was the only daughter of the house, Maman needed me here. And though I am so poor at it, until Gratien marries, he still needs me here as his hostess——' she stopped, throwing a hesitant glance at Paula. 'I am talking too much about myself. You should not encourage me.'

'If I did, it was because I am interested. And I'm wondering whether you would show me some of your work some time?' asked Paula.

'I should be glad to,' Louise agreed readily. 'But you will find it very amateur.'

On that they parted, Paula returning to her room, and pondering as she went the small tragedy which the older girl had revealed. What a difference between earnest, thwarted Louise and headstrong, guileful Monique! Which brought Paula back with a jolt to the thought of Monique's enforced admissions, her intrigue and her threats. Paula knew the latter to be no more than the flung defiance of Monique's desperate need for self-protection from the folly which she daren't allow to be known. She couldn't really harm Paula with them. And yet Paula found herself flinching from the prospect of Gratien de Tourcy's judgment of her failure to mention Barbizon; of ever having to ask him to take her word against Monique's. The same pride which had forbidden her to plead with Madame Sallust would operate again, though with the difference that she had not cared at all for either Antoine or Annick Sallust's opinion of her, whereas she was already too aware of Gratien's challenge to her to be coolly indifferent to his. No, deplore Monique's tactics as she might, she had to go along with them. One careless slip of either of their tongues, and Monique would be in the trouble she was prepared to lie to avoid, and Paula herself would, at best, have some awkward explanations to make.

When she went downstairs an hour later Gratien was in the hall, looking through some letters. He excused himself to her while he made a short telephone call, then took her into the salon, a long gracious room with floor-to-ceiling windows at either end. It was furnished with antiques, shining cabinets and bureaux and graceful chairs covered and cushioned in old damask. Paula admired the flower arrangements, saying she understood they were by Louise, and Gratien agreed, 'Yes, she is happier using her hands and dealing with things rather than with people. Which is why, as you may notice while you are here, I take over from her some of the tasks a more confident hostess might prefer to handle herself. For instance, I doubt whether you, or anyone in your place, would have been here today if I hadn't taken charge of an interview which, when I arrived, seemed about to die on its feet.'

Paula said demurely, as she felt she was expected to, 'I'm glad it didn't.'

'So shall we be, one hopes.' He asked then how she had found her quarters, whether she had met the staff, and brought to her the drink she chose. Tall enough to rest an elbow on the high mantelshelf, he remained standing with his own drink, looking down at her as he said, 'Perhaps it's not too early to ask what you know on the subject of wine, Miss Raymond?'

33

'Do you mean in a general way, or in connection with my job?' she asked.

'Both. About wine from the grape to bottle, and the civilised use of it when it's there.'

'Well, about grapevines and processing and maturing, not very much.'

'Though while you are in the heart of the wine region, you'd be willing to learn?'

'I'd be very glad to, if I have time.'

'We must see that time is made for you. And the rest?'

'About wine in relation to food? Yes, I hope I'm fairly knowledgeable about that.'

'And so—at a dinner-party where the main dish is to be, say, *entrecôte bordelaise*, what wine would you choose to serve with that course?'

Paula flushed. 'You want me to name a vintage? I'm afraid I'm no connoisseur.'

'A type, then?'

'Well, with red meat, a red wine of some body, and in this part of France a claret, although——'

'Yes—although?' he prompted.

She raised her eyes full to his. 'I was going to say that if there were a host for the dinner-party, as merely his caterer I should expect *him* to make the choice of wines and tell *me* what to serve!'

He laughed aloud at that, throwing back his head, and hearing the depth of his laugh and watching the taut-drawn muscles of his throat, Paula was suddenly aware of his physical appeal to her senses. It was an unfamiliar sensation; a little unbalancing. Usually her response to other people's attraction came second to her liking them, and in answer to their liking for her. It was a new experience to feel the pull of the magnetism of a man who was concerned only with her value to him as an employee; new and disturbing and futile as an experience, and with no future to it at all.

As comment upon what had evoked his laughter, he said, 'If your catering matches your diplomacy in the face of awkward questions, you should go far, Miss Raymond. Put your mind to it, and you can probably make a fine art of both of them.' Then, partly changing the subject, 'Meanwhile, when we both find ourselves with some free time, I'll have you instructed in the basics of choosing an acceptable wine, even when you are lacking a host!'

Dinner, after they had been joined by the others, was a simple affair of vichyssoise soup, cold poached salmon served with a dry white wine, followed by a dessert of fresh fruit. The talk was mostly of plans for the coming weeks.

Milon asked whether there was a horse in the stables which he might ride. Monique, on hearing that Gratien would be compiling his guest list and sending out the invitations from his office, offered eagerly to help.

'I do have a secretary,' he reminded her.

'Yes, but—Besides, while you and I were doing it together, you could tell me about the people you are asking, and that would make it easier for me to make small talk with them at meals. Please, Gratien, do let me help!' she urged.

'And how do you know you are going to be among those present when I'm engaged in conning my guests on the superiority of de Tourcy wines? You may well find yourself banished to the nursery wing for cocoa and omelette suppers,' he teased her.

She frowned at that. 'Gratien, that's twice since we arrived that you've tried to pretend you think I'm still a child! When are you going to realise that at eighteen, one is grown-up?'

He fingered the stem of his wine glass. 'Perhaps, say, when I have to play the heavy host and lock you away from the attentions of unsuitable young men?' he offered.

'Pouf! You needn't bother. I don't mostly like young men. I much prefer older ones—at least thirty, and experienced.'

Gratien laughed. 'Famous Last Words—and I do believe you think they are original!'

Monique flushed and looked down at her plate. 'Oh, if you can't be serious——' she muttered. At which point it seemed that Louise thought it time to intervene.

'Now I was hoping, dear, that you might like to learn something about cooking and entertaining from Miss Raymond. I'm sure she would be glad for you to watch her at work, and when she goes marketing, to let you go along.' As Monique turned wide, affronted eyes upon her, Louise's resolution appeared to falter. 'Though only—well, only when you had nothing better to do, of course. But I did just think that your mother would like you to know something about such things for the time when you marry. Just an idea I had, that's all.'

In face of Monique's continuing stare, her voice trailed away. Monique said, 'Thank you, Louise. But Maman says one needn't trouble about that sort of thing, so long as one marries reasonably well. It's much more important, Maman says, to keep one's husband's interest and desire alive, than to be dabbling in the kitchen all the time. Besides,' her glance now fixed on Paula, 'during my last term at Barbizon we did have a woman who was supposed to lecture us on cooking and food values. But we used to skip her sessions as often as we could. It was all so *boring*, and she left before the end of term. In some kind of disgrace, we heard. But we weren't told the details.'

For a long moment Paula returned the stare, then looked away, despising the pettiness of the girl's revenge. She thought Monique had probably enjoyed telling the story, knowing that by mentioning no names, she ran no risk. But Paula, disgusted at being made the butt of such oblique malice, resolved to take Monique to task as soon as they found themselves alone.

She asked Gratien when the actual harvesting of the grapes would begin, and he told her, 'In this region the gathering is ordered by decree by public proclamation from the Tour du Roy in St Emilion. In 1199 your English King John gave its Jurade the freedom to make its own laws for St Emilion, and this year it is to be next week that the members of the Jurade announce the *Ban des Vendanges*—proclaim the vintage—from the tower of the king's castle. It's a ceremony we all attend; you must see it too.'

Paula said she would like to. Monique said she had seen it before, and it was just an excuse for a lot of middle-aged men to dress up and sound important, but as it seemed to be the done thing, she would probably go along too. Gratien would be driving, wouldn't he, so could she go with him?

Gratien said, 'I'm sorry, but I shall be taking a couple of colleagues. Milon can drive you and Miss Raymond and Louise, if she wants to go, in the car we're putting at Miss Raymond's disposal for doing her shopping in Libourne. We might meet for luncheon in the town, but don't count on it. It will be a business day for me.'

It was later, as they were on their way up to their rooms, that Paula had her chance with Monique, when Milon went on ahead to his.

Paula said curtly, 'That was pretty silly of you at dinner. You know what I mean?'

Monique shrugged. 'Perhaps. But I was tempted to give you a foretaste of what I *could* say, if I ever had to suspect you of giving me away.'

'Well, it was totally unnecessary——'

Monique's black eyes glinted. 'You mean there's no risk at all that you would ever tell on me to Gratien?'

'None whatsoever that I can see. Why should I?' Paula queried.

'I don't know.' Monique bit her lip in thought. 'Unless—well, you did try to put me off Gratien, and if you thought he was getting too interested in me, you might——'

'And what would it matter to me how interested he might become, do you suppose?'

'Perhaps if you ever envied me the attentions he was paying me; if, for instance, you'd begun to get romantic ideas about him yourself?'

38

'Look,' said Paula crossly, 'he employs me; I am here for just six weeks on a job which promises to be pretty demanding, and one happens to need time and a fair amount of intimacy for falling in love, didn't you know?'

'Well, Louise seems to be providing the intimacy for you—treating you like one of us. And in six weeks a lot can happen. It has to, for me,' said Monique, as she turned away, leaving Paula to remember her own momentary sensual attraction to Gratien. Of course it had nothing to do with the kind of love which mattered and lasted, and it hadn't been returned; Gratien de Tourcy had shown no such interest in her. But she had to wonder whether her irritation had betrayed to Monique her brief awareness of him as a man; whether, supposing she had laughed off the girl's jealous suggestion with a light, 'You must be joking!' her denial would have carried enough conviction to allay Monique's suspicions of herself as a competitor for Gratien's interest. Privately Paula thought it would be strange if, at thirty-two, wealthy and as yet unmarried, he was as readily there for the snaring as Monique seemed to hope. There must have been—were now —would be, women in his circle who could outbid Monique in the matter of charm and poise and social standing any day. From which Paula went on to wonder what type of woman had appeal for him —and then was again annoyed with herself for caring to know.

Breakfast, it appeared, was not taken communally. Paula's coffee and rolls were brought to her room quite early by Rosalie, and afterwards Paula went downstairs through a house which, except for the hum of distant vacuum cleaners and the chink of crockery from the kitchens, was silent and deserted. She herself had dressed for work in the kitchen, in a tailored white overall with very short cuffed sleeves and a broad white bandeau for her hair. Knee-length white kid boots, extravagantly expensive but of a texture as soft as a glove, completed a uniform which she liked to regard as her signature tune.

She had been prepared for some opposition in the kitchen, having sometimes encountered it before in her freelancing days when resident staff had, understandably, resented the temporary incursion and supervision of a stranger. But here she was welcomed. Emilie the cook was clearly glad to be relieved of the full responsibility for the *haute cuisine* menus required by the de Tourcys for their guests when they arrived, and she ruled her young assistants with a rod of discipline which had them murmuring an instant 'M'dame' of obedience and scurrying immediately about any errand or job she had for them. And even on that first morning, when they were both out of earshot, she confided to Paula, 'They are good children, and of course one sees how it is with them. They are sweethearts and they keep each other attentive to their work, lest I complain to Mademoiselle and one of them is sent packing, leaving the other behind. Pierre wants to become a pastrycook and buy his own shop one day. Ah——' Emilie lifted her hands in a wide gesture—'ambition and love, they are very good things for the young to enjoy when they happen hand-in-hand.'

Paula had brought down with her a collection of the French and English cookbooks which were her favourites in use, and she and Emilie pored over them for a while, comparing preferences and dislikes, successes and failures. Paula was being instructed on some particular regional dishes she would be expected to serve when Gratien came through from the courtyard.

He was in riding-breeches and an open-necked shirt, and Emilie showed no surprise at sight of him in her domain. 'Ah, m'sieur—your coffee as usual?' she asked, and at his nod, went to pour a cup from a percolator on a stove. He greeted Paula and took the cup. 'Emilie expects me to call in for this, whenever I've been out on an early-morning ride,' he explained. Resting long-leggedly against a table-edge, he sipped the coffee and chatted with Emilie, then brought his glance back to Paula.

Between sips, 'You look very functional—as if you meant business,' he remarked.

'Thank you,' she said.

'And when are we going to be allowed to sample your art? Or is it a science nowadays—I've never known?'

She answered that question first. 'It's a bit of both, I think,' she said. 'And I hope Emilie will let me try my hand as soon as she has introduced me to all her equipment, and it has accepted me. And as soon as I have learnt some of the dishes which she tells me you all like.'

'You shouldn't trouble too much about that,' he

advised. 'We shall probably survive the ordeal, supposing you wish to experiment.'

'But I mean to,' she retorted with spirit. 'In fact, Emilie is all for my giving you some English food for a change.'

'Such as, for instance—Scotch broth and Irish stew and Welsh rarebit?' he asked ironically in English which brought a look of surprise from Paula.

'And steak-and-kidney pie, and eggs and bacon and plum duff, I daresay, too,' she answered him in the same language, and was surprised again when he translated the names of the dishes into their nearest equivalents in French for Emilie's benefit.

'You speak and understand English better than I expected,' Paula told him, back in French again now.

'Than you expected—from what?' he parried.

She hadn't supposed he would force her to explain the thought which had prompted her remark. But since he had—'Well, perhaps from the kind of prejudice you showed me, when you interviewed me for this post.' It had taken some moral courage to say it, and the short laugh with which he brushed it off was almost an affront.

'My dear girl,' he scoffed, still in English, 'that was my native reaction to all I have suffered at the hands of your country's run-of-the-mill habits in eating and drinking, and I gave you the chance to prove me wrong, didn't I? As for my English—the wine industry is a cosmopolitan affair; one needs to be all things to all men in German, English, Italian —the lot, when one is the salesman and they are the buyers, and they know their job as well as one hopes one knows one's own.' He put down his cup and told Emilie, 'You needn't send up *café complet* for me. I'll skip it this morning, as I've had some coffee.' He turned at the door on his way out.

'When did you plan to reconnoitre Libourne or St Emilion with a view to your marketing?' he asked Paula.

'I don't know. Whenever it is convenient,' she answered.

'For you to have the runabout? Well, any time for that. But I'd rather you didn't drive it alone the first time. I'll get Milon to take you—probably to Libourne, as it is nearer and bigger than St E. Say at three—after the shops' midday closing?' After her 'Thank you' of agreement he went out, leaving her to question her irrational wish that he had offered to escort her himself. It must be, she supposed, because she half-enjoyed the verbal battle to which he seemed always able to goad her. It certainly had nothing in common with that momentary magnetic pull which she had experienced in relation to him. This was a poles-apart thing of argument and counter-argument; a healthy friction of their points of view; nothing emotional to it at all, whch made it infinitely less ... dangerous.

When she went out to the garages in the afternoon, expecting to meet Milon there, it was Gratien instead who was awaiting her at the wheel of a small open car.

'I found Milon wanted to go riding,' he explained, 'so I'm taking you myself.'

43

On the way, 'How far is Libourne?' she asked.

'Not more than twelve kilometres; St Emilion about eight. Both easy level roads, though St Emilion town stands on a hilltop.' He turned to look at her, his glance noting the sleeveless sunflower-patterned dress into which she had changed, and the black-and-yellow kerchief tied gipsy fashion with the knot over one ear.

'You only need a basket, a deeper tan and some hoop ear-rings to pass for a genuine Romany,' he remarked, and before she could reply, 'I suppose that's why fancy-dress affairs are more popular with women than with men; they know the value of a complete change of costume for investing them with a new personality.'

'Do they?'

'Well, don't they? For instance, a nurse in plain clothes is just another pretty girl: in her bibbed white starch she becomes a radiant ministering angel, no less.'

Paula thought about it. 'And a woman dentist in *her* white starched coat?' she posed demurely.

Gratien laughed. 'You shouldn't have such a logical mind. In any case the comparison doesn't hold. One expects to be hurt by a dentist; one hopes to be cured by a nurse, and it colours the image remarkably. In favour of the nurse, of course.'

'Of course.' Emboldened by his having brought up the subject, she went on, 'And women cooks in their uniform and out of it—what about them?'

Quickly he glanced at her again. 'I knew you would have to ask that. Trust any woman to reduce a discussion to the personal in a matter of minutes!

However, since you ask—out of her starch she is human enough to be vulnerable to criticism; in it she is clinical, formidable, and as her employer, one has to hope she is as efficient as she looks.'

Paula sat up very straight and looked fixedly ahead. 'Thank you. As long as we know,' she said. (Verbal banter? That was all? Then why was she slightly a-tremble with this nervous excitement, as if the fanciful exchange were really deeply personal, its outcome of importance to them both?)

After a silence she changed the subject to suggest that if she were to use the car, she should try driving it now. But he told her No. They were almost into the town, and she should drive it on the return journey.

Between the château and Libourne the river had taken a great bend in its course, as if to accommodate the town also on its banks. There was a fine riverside promenade and a wide-spanned bridge and a centre town of ancient streets and an arcaded principal square. Most of the shops had reopened after the traditional noonday closing of the south, and Gratien took Paula and introduced her to several where the château kept running accounts. She thought he would have bypassed the modern supermarkets if she hadn't insisted on looking them over too.

'I don't think Louise shops much at them,' he demurred.

'Never mind. They often have bargains for cash. The street markets too. Which is market-day here?' she asked.

'Every day. Do you want to sample them as well?'

45

'Please.'

He followed her tolerantly as she wandered, fascinated as always by the sheer complexity of the goods on sale in a French market—tawdry ornaments cheek-by-jowl with genuine antiques; piled fruit and flowers; cheeses, fish, toys, clothes, crockery and garden tools, wine—all in good-tempered competition with each other and all selling well.

Paula had stopped to price some Roquefort cheeses and behind her Gratien was saying, 'We aren't putting you on a tight budget, you know——' when they both heard his name called, and they both turned about.

'Solange!' Both hands offered to her, he stepped forward to greet the girl who had called to him and who now saluted him with a kiss on either cheek.

'Gratien!' She stood back from him. 'It must be a year since——'

'A week this way or that, yes,' he agreed. 'You are staying with the Montdorets again?'

'As usual. Julien and Clara keep open house for the vintage, as you know. You'll be coming over?'

'And you to us. We shall see you at St E. next week, no doubt?'

In the background Paula had time to study the newcomer, struck by her prettiness which was that of a life-sized doll—round face, round dimpled chin, blue eyes, high cheekbones stained with a rosy flush, blonde hair strained back from her face into a heavy knot at her nape. Figure, narrow hands, slim legs and feet were all in perfect proportion.

Gratien introduced them. 'Solange—Miss Raymond, our English caterer—Mademoiselle Courtet, a guest of our neighbours at the Château Aragon.'

Solange Courtet offered a tiny hand. 'English? That is a novelty. The Montdorets have engaged a man this year—another innovation. Clara says it was because the rest of her staff were always hostile to a woman. Do you find you are resented too?' she asked Paula.

'On the contrary, Mademoiselle de Tourcy's staff seem very helpful,' said Paula.

'Then you are lucky.' As if that was all the conversation Paula was entitled to, Solange Courtet turned back to Gratien. 'I've got my car, and I suppose you have yours. If you've time, why not come back to Aragon now?'

'Not now. I have to take Miss Raymond back.'

She regarded him and Paula with a puzzled tilt of her head. 'Oh—you are together? You haven't just happened to meet in town?'

'No. I'm showing Miss Raymond the stores where she will be shopping, and handing over to her the car she'll be using while she is here. Perhaps, though, I'd be welcome at Aragon this evening instead?' Gratien offered.

A dimpled smile lit up the pretty doll face. 'Welcome? What do you suppose?' the rosebud lips said to him by way of parting as they shook hands.

That night at dinner, the first meal which Paula had helped to prepare, she did not need Louise's telling that Gratien would not be at home. She would have been surprised if he were. More than once since meeting Solange Courtet, she had been reminded of her own guess that Monique almost certainly had competitors for his attentions. She remembered having wondered too where his taste in women friends lay—wondered, and hadn't wanted the answers to matter.

But somehow he was sparking her interest too keenly for the answers not to matter. And if one answer were Solange Courtet's appeal for him, that mattered for reasons which had nothing to do with Monique.

CHAPTER THREE

'*Mon dieu*, is *she* here again?' Monique's reaction to Louise's explanation for Gratien's absence from dinner caused Louise to look pained.

'Solange Courtet, you mean, dear? Why, don't you like her?' she asked.

'Not particularly. Behind that baby-face she is as hard as nails. Besides, she is too rich, and sees that everyone knows how rich.'

From across the table Milon crooked a taunting forefinger at his sister. 'You are jealous, that's what,' he said, and Louise reproved gently, 'She can't help being the heiress to Courtet Frères, the shippers, and we always welcome her when she comes to stay with Julien and Clara Montdoret, who are two of our best friends. Gratien——'

'Oh, Gratien welcomes her all right!' Monique cut in. 'Though perhaps he can hardly help himself, the way she claims him on sight. Last year, whenever we went out together she always paired off with him, leaving Milon and me to trail in their wake like a couple of—pages. If she'd been wearing a train, I'd not have been surprised if she had expected us to carry it!'

'Well, that was Gratien's fault, if he didn't find some young people of your own age to partner you. And you can hardly wonder that Gratien and Solange like to spend time together. After all, we have

49

known her ever since she first came to stay at Aragon, when she was not long out of the schoolroom. Rather like yourself now, dear,' Louise offered brightly, as if she hoped the comparison would please, and when Monique's scowl showed that it did not, she turned to Paula.

'You met Mademoiselle Courtet this afternoon, didn't you? What did you think of her to look at? She is rather exquisite, is she not?'

'Of her type, very,' Paula agreed.

'Yes. Like fine, translucent china. Last year I tried to paint her, and though in colour she defeated me, I did a very passable sketch in black and white which I remember Gratien thought was good,' Louise mused. Then, head on one side, she scrutinised Paula. 'Perhaps I might attempt a drawing of you one day, Miss Raymond? You would allow me to?'

Paula laughed. 'I'd be no subject for you, I'm afraid. I'm too ordinary.'

Louise shook her head. 'Not so. Not so at all. You have an air ... a quality I should like to be able to catch. The English look, perhaps? Or, with your short hair, the look of a girl who would have made a charming boy, but who remains a girl for all that? If I could capture that—Yes, you must certainly let me try.'

After dinner Paula found herself briefly alone with Milon, who had barely addressed a word to her since they arrived. Now, not sounding as if he genuinely pitied Monique, he said lazily, 'My poor little sister; Gratien ... Gratien. Jealous of him and for him, she may be, but wouldn't you expect her to show more finesse?'

Paula said, 'I doubt if she is of an age yet to understand how to manipulate finesse——'

'Bah! I thought your sex was supposed to learn it in your cradles—at any rate, with regard to men,' he taunted.

'Some do. Some don't. And if I may say so,' Paula added, 'I don't think it helps for you to accuse her of jealousy in front of other people, however much in fun.'

'But jealousy is such a waste. Envy now—that's much more productive. Jealousy is at least half self-pity, but if you envy someone enough for what they've got and you haven't, you are more likely to go after some of it yourself.'

'Using fair means or foul?'

'Oh, fair of course, if they'll deliver the goods. If not——'

It was a fruitless conversation which did not endear Milon's outlook to Paula, but which she was to remember to some purpose later on.

The next day she got down to work in earnest. The first of the weekend house-guests were not due until after the proclamation of the vintage at St Emilion. But Paula laid her catering plans well ahead, checking the stores she would need, and having made sure she could command all the necessary ingredients, she drew up a set of suggested menus which she took to Louise for her approval.

Louise looked them over, murmuring hesitantly, 'Yes ... yes. The first luncheon *hors d'oeuvres*—

smoked ham. The fish course—crayfish tails in wine sauce. Fillet of pork with stuffed cabbage. And the cheeses—Brie. Auvergne Bleu. Yes ... yes.' She went through the list, consulting or questioning Paula on one or two points, then handed it back to her.

'You will show this to my brother, of course?'

'Before I go ahead with it?' asked Paula.

'Yes. For him to choose the wines accordingly. He always does that himself.' Louise smiled a little apologetically. 'It is our wines which we have to sell, you see. So you mustn't mind if Gratien cuts across some of your menus, for the reason that they wouldn't marry successfully with the wine he plans to serve.'

'I see,' said Paula, remembering his compliment on her diplomacy when she had put the ball back into his court by her suggestion that though the food was her business, the accompanying wines were his. So far, they were agreed. But she had gone to a lot of trouble in the compilation of the menus with which Louise had found no fault, and today, having ideas of her own as to the kind of wine they would match, she was prepared to do battle for some of them, should he claim that they wouldn't do.

It was as well that she had been warned. For though he approved some of her plans, his cutting across others amounted to a slashing which left gaping holes in her programme.

His blue pencil was active. 'Too heavy for a luncheon meal; forget one of the courses and serve fresh fruit for the dessert. For soup—a consommé rather than a crême: you have included no lamb, which is a great favourite in the region; a grill would be preferable to a roast here; and where among your cheeses is the Dutch?'

Paula looked her surprise. 'Dutch? Here? Where your own cheeses are world-famous?'

'Dutch,' he insisted. 'Though perhaps you couldn't be expected to know that we've favoured them since, in the eighteenth century, the Dutch ships carrying our wines abroad brought back their cheeses as ballast, and we serve them often because their mild taste sets off a full-bodied wine to advantage. Yes, some Dutch, please.' He wrote in 'Edam?' 'Gouda?' in place of some of Paula's suggestions and handed the papers back to her. 'They'll do, on the whole, and I expect you will be able to think again on the lines I've indicated,' he said.

Paula 'thought again'; leafed through her private records of dishes she had served which had proved singularly successful; filled in most of the gaps, and in the case of one main course which Gratien had scrapped completely, came to a rather impish decision about it. If he wanted to see her amended menus the joke would probably turn sour on her, but if he didn't question them again until he was ordering the wine for that meal it was going to be too late to serve anything else in place of—good English home-salted silverside, Norfolk dumplings, carrots in white sauce and the juices the meat had been boiled in for gravy!

Meanwhile the vineyards and the winery buildings were a-hum with activity, short of the actual cutting of the crop. The *douils*, the metal-banded tubs into which the cut grapes would be loaded, were massed in the cellar courtyards; the last of the great fermentation casks were being cleaned at the cellar entrances. The machinery of the *égrappoirs*, the crushing vats, was being tested, and the casual workers who would do the bulk of the gathering were beginning to arrive, the early ones in caravans which they would make their homes for the duration of the vintage, the later ones by car and moped and mule-cart to take up the quarters and cooking facilities provided for them in the estate's outbuildings.

The air of expectancy was infectious; the gossip was all of the value of the vintage and of the weather, since a lashing rain storm or a freak early frost could wreak havoc in the crop in an hour or two overnight. St Emilion's celebration of the *Ban des Vendanges* couldn't come too soon . . .

The ceremony was in the morning; the rest of the day was given over to holiday mood, with a fair and sports and street sideshows. Milon drove the runabout with Paula and Monique as passengers, and Louise who, after wavering as to whether she would or would not go, finally went.

It was Paula's first visit to St Emilion and she was enchanted with the little town on its hillside, surrounded garden-wise by its neat vineyards; the mellowed gold of its ancient buildings in contrasting harmony with the seas of green.

It had been a *bastide*, a fortified walled town. Its streets were narrow, its walls were thick and its ruins had an age-old dignity. Now it was wholly given over to the cultivation of its grapes, of which there was an all-pervading scent in its streets, filled to capacity today by foot-shuffling, hilarious, cat-calling crowds.

The members of the Jurade—Monique's 'dressed-up middle-aged men'—in scarlet robes and white hoods marched in formal procession, followed by a rabble of children and dogs, to the great pile of the King's Tower of the twelfth-century castle, where after some complicated ceremonial, the proclamation of the opening of the vintage was duly made. There would be a corresponding celebration in May, Paula learned, for the fêting of the spring and the tasting of the new wine which this autumn's harvest had produced.

The audience dispersed, the tourists to their coaches for sightseeing in the town and the natives to the cafés and sideshows, to meet their neighbours and to toast the vintage in robust St Emilion 'red'. The de Tourcy party choose a restaurant shaded by gay canopies which so darkened the interior that, coming in from the noon sunshine, they had been shown to a table before they noticed that the nearest table for four was occupied by Gratien, the girl whom Paula recognised as Solange Courtet and a man and woman she did not know.

Under her breath Monique muttered, 'And he said it was a *business* day for him!' as both men rose and Louise crossed to the other table to chat. Presently she beckoned the three young people over, mentioned that the others already knew Milon and Monique, and introduced Paula to the Comte and Comtesse Montdoret, as 'Miss Raymond, our caterer for the vintage. She is English,' causing Paula to brace herself for the slightly incredulous echo to which by now she was becoming used. But neither the Comte nor the Comtesse, a dumpy figure in a countrified hat, made it. The Comte bowed formally and his wife extended a plump hand. 'Welcome to the region, mademoiselle,' she said. 'Is it your first visit to our wine country—either on holiday, or to work?'

Paula said it was, though it was not her first visit to France. She had studied and worked elsewhere for over three years, whereupon the Comte intervened to congratulate her on her command of French, and after a few more pleasantries she and the others returned to their table.

But both tables were close enough for the talk sometimes to be general, and drawn into most of the discussions as she was by the Mondorets' friendly geniality, Paula found herself entirely at ease. Towards the end of the meal Louise announced that they meant to show Paula the historic sights before they returned to the château, agreeing with the chorused suggestions as to all the antiquities she must not miss—the ruins of the Cardinal's Palace, the Cordelier Cloisters, the villas of the Gallo-Roman era, the watchman's tower, the monolithic church hewn out of a single massive rock—'And of *course* St Emilion's Hermitage,' claimed Clara Montdoret with odd emphasis and a knowing nod.

'But of course,' Louise agreed with, for her, unwonted decision. 'We certainly must not allow her to miss that.'

Paula looked from one to the other with a smile. 'It sounds as if there is something very special about the Hermitage. Is there?' she asked.

The spread of the Comtesse's fat hands was expressive. 'But indeed! That is, for anyone in your case, mademoiselle, *very* special indeed!'

'In my case?' Paula puzzled aloud, aware as she spoke of Monique's scowl and of Solange Courtet's light voice claiming,

'Let's all go to the Hermitage! Shall we? May we?' Her hand on Gratien's arm added emphasis to her plea.

His glance at her was indulgent. 'You went last year, with singularly little result,' he reminded her.

She wrinkled her pretty nose at him. 'All the more reason why I should try again this year! When the others go, to take Miss Raymond, will you take me too? Besides, I meant to go today because——' she tapped her bag, 'I brought the necessary along.'

Gratien agreed, 'Very well, if Clara and Julien will wait for you until I bring you back.'

The Montdorets said they would, and though Monique grumbled that it was a silly waste of time, she went along too when a move was made.

The eighth-century chapel of the anchorite St Emilion was a cave-like building in the centre of the town, a place of rough-hewn arches of barely more than head-height, a stone altar, a stone seat, a stone bed hollowed out to the shape of a coffin, and a wall-fountain gushing into a shallow stone tray. Paula stood with Gratien and Louise, awed by the austerity of the place and accustoming her eyes to its gloom. Solange waited until a laughing group of young people moved away from the fountain, then went to it, beckoning to Gratien as she did so. 'Come and see,' she called to him while she fumbled in her bag.

'What is it? What happens?' Paula asked Louise as they followed him.

'Just a piece of folklore the local girls believe,' Louise told her. 'You throw two pins into the water, and if the force of the swirl makes them cross each other in the form of an X before they reach the outflow, then you will be married before the year is out.'

Amused, 'And do they ever cross of their own accord?' Paula asked.

Louise smiled. 'More often than not, I hear they don't. But——'

'Well, mine had better, this time,' threatened Solange as she held a pin between each forefinger and thumb and dropped them into the water. 'I've often wondered whether weighting their heads would help,' she mused, as they all watched the pins rock to and fro, turn point to point, then head to head, before a gentle lap of the water laid one of them across the other to the sound of an ecstatic yelp from Solange.

'There! Who said I didn't get results?' she triumphed at Gratien, who said, 'Congratulations. Who is to be the happy man? Or haven't you chosen him yet?'

Solange dimpled. 'Perhaps he doesn't know ʸᵉᵗ he has chosen *me*. He has a whole year in which ᵗᵒ make up his mind, after all. I needn't hurry him. I can afford to wait.'

She had snatched up the pins from the water and

now handed them to Paula. 'Your turn next,' she said. '*Bonne chance!*'

Paula played along with the whimsy. 'Are there any rules as to how one should drop them in?' she asked.

'No. Follow your fancy.' So Paula dropped them both together, watched them separate, run parallel towards the vortex of the outflow where, just as they were about to be engulfed, one turned at an angle to form a distinct cross with its fellow before they were both swept away.

'There—just in time. Are you engaged?' asked Solange.

'No.'

'Oh well, you've plenty of time, as I have.' Solange turned to Monique. 'Sorry, I've no more pins.'

Monique shrugged. 'It doesn't matter. It's a stupid superstition anyway.'

But there Louise interposed. 'No, Monique dear, it's just a piece of fun for you young people. Here——' she fumbled beneath the lapel of her jacket—'I have some pins. Try.'

Monique snatched the pins, tossed them into the water from the distance at which she stood, and they all watched as both pins took a direct channel towards the outflow and disappeared.

Monique said nothing. Louise murmured, 'Oh dear, perhaps I shouldn't have——' But her gallant effort to take the blame for the pins' failure to co-operate did nothing to disperse Monique's ill-humour, and Gratien's brisk, 'Well, Solange and I will leave you to the rest of Miss Raymond's sightseeing,' decisively broke up a party upon which embarrassment had suddenly come down.

Paula, seeing Solange's arm tucked intimately into Gratien's as they went out to his car, felt irritated with Monique's churlishness, but she was sorry for the girl too. Jealousy, as Milon had said with shrewd cynicism, was a terrible waste of spirit. But was anyone ever strong-minded enough to recognise and fight the shrivelling effect of its gall? Monique, frightened of Solange's rivalry, evidently couldn't. Could she herself, Paula wondered, if ever she were given deep cause?

If ever—? Suddenly the question was demandingly here and now, and though the answer wasn't that she was jealous of either Monique or Solange, she knew with too-cruel honesty that she was at one with Monique in a common purpose—that they both coveted the interest of the same man.

But how had it happened—that in a few days a trivial physical attraction had turned to a craving to be known, to be wanted, to be invited to share everything about Gratien de Tourcy which would never be hers to enjoy at his hands, since he had given her no cause to hope that he had any such answering thought about her? She was twenty-five; she loved her work, though not to the total exclusion of relationships with men; she had been wooed, and had responded to a point. But never before had her own desire gone in headlong pursuit of a man she hardly knew ... who scarcely knew her.

This was madness. In a few weeks' time she would be no more to him than one of the much-quoted 'ships in the night' passing by. As many months more, and she would be 'that English girl we engaged for last year's vintage'. For her too, her brief stay under his roof would have become a bittersweet interlude, best forgotten. Meanwhile, she had to cope with their everyday contacts, and keep her secret for dignity's sake.

Crossed pins in a fountain indeed! Marriage for her within a year! The wry humour of it struck her and helped to restore her balance. After Gratien, what handsome young Lochinvar riding unexpectedly out of the West was going to have any appeal for her at all? After Gratien——

Following that day at St Emilion work became paramount. That weekend's guests—a party of three German wine-buyers, a journalist and a Paris restaurateur and his wife—arrived to be fêted and their influence unobtrusively wooed in the future interests of the de Tourcy cellars. The men enjoyed a day's shooting and toured the vineyards; Louise, shy, and Monique, bored, entertained Madame Leclerc and Paula and the kitchen staff were at full stretch, serving food to Paula's design and the accompanying wines to Gratien's choice, dictated to Paula some time before each meal.

It was for the Sunday evening's dinner that she had planned her typically English course and she was prepared for the defensive when she handed him the menu she proposed.

'M'm.' He looked it over. 'With the paté, a dry white Graves, I think. With the——' He glanced up, brows raised. 'What's this?'

61

'The salt beef? You'll remember you didn't care for what I'd suggested there, so I made another choice. And I wrote it in English because it sounds better that way,' she told him.

'I see. And you've prepared it already?'

'It's in course of preparation. Simmering the beef takes a long time.'

'And what precisely is a Norfolk dumpling?'

She loved the accent which marked his English. 'In French it would be a *chausson*. You wouldn't expect "Norfolk" to be translatable any more than, say, "the Médoc" or "Auvergne" would be,' she said.

'No.' Silence. Then, 'This was deliberate on your part, wasn't it?'

The corner of her mouth twitched in a half-smile. 'Yes,' she said.

'A thumb-to-the-nose at me for my disparagement of the English *cuisine*?'

'A—sort of lesson, I thought, to show your guests that we don't necessarily tolerate mutton that's as tough as horse, nor soups which should be poured away down the drain.'

'Very well. Then I demand that you come to the table and teach us this lesson yourself. You'll dine with my guests tonight.'

She stared, taken aback. 'But when you are entertaining, you know I eat from a tray in my room. Besides, I have to be in the kitchen to the point where each course is sent to the table.'

'You must arrange for Emilie to take over to-night. When you take up a crusade you must be prepared to stand by your cause. You'll dine,' he said.

She went to bed that night, a little heady with success. Emilie, told of Gratien's edict and its reason, had co-operated wonderfully, and Paula, recalling a famous woman gastronome's tenet that to cook in evening dress was only a matter of well-learnt habits and intelligence, had changed into a black velvet blouson and pantalon skirt in the last quarter of an hour she had had at her disposal before she supervised the final preparations for the meal, and had reached the dining-room just in time.

After that, she had enjoyed every minute of her evening. Louise, shy as she was, was a good hostess, in that she tried to draw everyone out, setting various conversational balls rolling while contributing little herself. The Germans spoke both French and English fluently, and the general talk ran from one subject to another with ease.

Paula had been afraid that Gratien might force her to 'stand by her cause' by making an anecdote of their clash. But he had made no reference to it. The main course, as perfectly cooked and served as she could have wished, was apparently enjoyed by everyone; Madame Leclerc congratulated Louise upon it; Louise disowned praise which she said Paula, not she, had earned, and Gratien's indirect comment had been in the wine he had chosen to accompany it.

The connoisseurs round the table went into their appreciative routine. Gratien had been asked, 'One of your own?'

He had nodded. 'Yes, a '61. You approve?'

'A great wine!'

'Superb!'

'Good. I must say'—he had glanced at Paula as he spoke—'I chose it, seeing it as a worthy complement to Miss Raymond's catering——'

'And the dish is a worthy complement to *it*!' put in an enthusiast, with a stiff bow in Paula's direction.

'Thank you. And from another aspect,' Gratien went on, 'you'll probably understand that the region needs to dress its windows with the best it has to show this year, in view of our fairly recent—embarrassments.'

Monsieur Leclerc toyed with the stem of his glass. 'You mean—the scandals? But you weren't involved?'

'No. None of the reputable châteaux were. But it's possible it could have happened to any of us, and it tarnished our image badly.'

'What did? What scandals are you talking about?' It had been Milon who asked the question.

Gratien turned to him. 'Don't you read your newspaper?'

'Only the funnies and the sports pages.'

'Well, this was alleged fraud on a considerable scale. It couldn't be wholly proved, because no expert can swear to a wine's region of origin either by taste or analysis or by any other method. But it was fairly certain that inferior wines from Provence and Languedoc were going out from here under the Bordeaux controlled appellation labels, and now that almost all our wines are château-bottled on our own vineyards, to the extent that the thing was going on, we were all suspect.'

'You mean—of bringing cheap wines up from wherever else, and sending them out as genuine Bordeaux?' asked Milon, interested. 'An inside job, in fact? But how could it be done?'

Gratien shrugged. 'Bribery, one supposes. A corruptible clerk with access to stock records; a woman labeller in need of money. The bottle contents from a vineyard that had already won approval wouldn't be checked or questioned until they reached the buyers or the public and complaints of quality were lodged. Which was what happened a season or two back, and we are still living it down, though it isn't happening now.'

'But still—easy money for some, until the fraud was blown? And not too difficult to work, at that?'

'As you say, not too difficult, given a vineyard-owner who'd be fool enough to risk the neck of his reputation,' Gratien agreed. 'The controlling authorities always catch up, sooner than later.' Then he dropped the subject by turning to put a question to Madame Leclerc.

And so, for Paula, the evening had ended with the men being left to their brandy and cigars, when Paula had excused herself from adjourning to the salon to await them. Instead she had gone to the kitchen to congratulate Emilie and to free her and her young helpers to go home, and then had gone to her room, feeling that for the moment all was well with her world.

She hadn't undressed at once, and when she began to do so, she remembered she had dropped her evening pochette at the dining-table and had forgotten to retrieve it. Before she had left the kitchen she knew the men had joined the ladies in the salon, so the dining-room would be empty if she went down.

She found her bag had been picked up and left on a side-table, and she had been on her way back to her room with it when Gratien came out of the salon to cross the hall. He saw her and spoke as she had one foot on the first stair and a hand on the newel-post.

'Why don't we do it again some time?' he asked cryptically.

She had guessed what he meant, but pretended she didn't.

'Do what?' she had asked.

'Marry the perfect gourmet dish with a perfect gourmet wine and sit back and enjoy the result,' he said.

She had laughed. 'You took rather a chance, didn't you, in arranging the marriage? The food might have been a ghastly failure.'

'It was a risk I was prepared to take, and you didn't let me down,' he said coolly.

'Thank you.' She had turned then to go on her way, but he had called after her, 'Remember, we've made a date,' and when she had looked back, he had added, 'For cementing the Anglo-French alliance with another marriage as successful as tonight's.'

Which was why Paula took a happy euphoria into her dreams. It was his first direct and unstinted praise of her and a generous disavowal of his prejudice. She felt rewarded, warmed. At this outset of realising she loved him, she ought to be able to ask more than his praise of the work he employed her to do. But while its glow remained with her, it was enough.

CHAPTER FOUR

BETWEEN one set of the château's weekend guests and the next Paula was to find that she enjoyed comparative leisure, though it was indeed only by comparison with the hectic rush of the weekends. She had some time to herself and time to do her 'homework' of planning menus and then of searching the markets of Libourne and St Emilion for the ingredients she needed, which she enjoyed.

The fish – pike, salmon trout, crayfish, perch— being mostly freshwater, were novel to her. The French game season was open and she was able to chose hare and woodcock and the partridges which had almost disappeared recently from the English shops. She bought for salmis and pâtés, and for vegetable entrées of stuffed mushrooms and marinated beetroot, and for roasts of Pauillac lamb and Landes gosling and Bayonne ham baked in a pastry case, and for desserts of St Emilion macaroons, honey gâteaux and chestnut biscuits. Throughout the week the family ate simply, of soups and salads and grills which were mainly Emilie's province. But at the weekend Emilie willingly deferred to Paula's direction, and the four of them—Paula, Emilie, young Rosalie and Pierre—worked together in a harmonious team. Paula had not again attempted to slip in an English course; Gratien's 'date' for that was an invitation for which she was prepared to wait.

She did not see very much of either Milon or Monique. Milon rode or went hare-shooting or borrowed the runabout when she was not using it, and Monique, having firmly sidestepped Louise's suggestion that she should accompany or learn from Paula, spent most of the time he allowed her with Gratien, either in his office or driving out with him or about the estate. She was so blatant in her pursuit of him that Paula wondered whether she had ever heard of the tactic known as 'playing hard to get'. Certainly she did not make use of it where Gratien was concerned. Wherever he was, she was not very far away; her desperation in forcing him to accept her at her own value of herself as a woman having the opposite effect, Paula suspected. In the first week or so of the few Monique had claimed she had at her disposal, she seemed to have gained no romantic ground with him. He remained as coolly urbane with her as he showed himself with Paula. And *that* was no sign of latent ardour on his part, Paula could have told her. His mental dismissal of both of them as subjects for either honourable or dishonourable intentions could hardly have been more marked.

It was during that first interlude of Paula's leisure that Louise returned to her suggestion of wanting to sketch her. Paula again demurred that she wasn't worth the time and trouble. But Louise, for once insistent, got her way and posed her in various everyday situations—reading on a chaise-longue, looking out of a window and in her full uniform rig of white overall, bandeau and boots, with floury hands deep in a pastry-mixing bowl at a kitchen table. The first two Louise gave her, keeping the other to work up from the rough of her pencil attempt, by enlarging and elaborating it in pastel chalks and giving it some background. If she could do it as she envisaged it, it would be a novel addition to her portfolio, she claimed.

'Not that I am ever likely to show *that* to much purpose now,' she added wistfully. 'It is too late.'

But Paula was to be charmed with the result. Louise's drawing was of the impressionist school—economical of line, its effects suggested by inspired use of light and shade. Behind Paula's figure at the table Louise had caught perfectly the contrast between the antique of the stone arches and the modern of the twentieth-century kitchen paraphernalia, just as Paula's rather space-age uniform was in contrast to the age-old craft of kneading dough by hand.

'You like it?' Louise inquired anxiously.

'Very much.'

'I showed it to Gratien and he liked it too. I said I'd thought of titling it *A Cook For Our Times*, but he suggested *L'Entente Cordiale* would be better.'

Paula took a moment to think that out. 'But to anyone who didn't know that I was English, working in a French château's kitchen, that wouldn't mean much,' she said.

'No,' Louise agreed. 'I felt he was thinking more of the way you yourself have begun to fit in here, rather than of the impersonal French-English aspect of just any English cook in any French kitchen, do you know?'

'Did he say so?' asked Paula, savouring the little

secret pleasure known to every girl in love, of discussing her man as impassively as she would speak of a stranger.

Louise said, 'No. But I'm sure that's how he was thinking.' Beginning to riffle among the litter of papers, drawing materials, manilla folders and paperweights weighing down nothing, which crowded her studio desk, she went on, 'Now I'd like to give you the original sketch I made, if you'd care to have it as you have the others. But I can't find it—yet I thought I had kept it. Yes, of course I would have kept it, knowing I meant you to have it. But where——?'

She peered into a folder, sent a pile of papers glissading, extracted the contents of another folder, dropped them and put a hand to her head as Paula knelt to gather them and return them to her.

'I really am the most inept creature,' Louise despaired. 'Do you know that not a day passes but that I lose something, or forget something or pay bills twice over, or don't pay them at all? I can't think how or why Gratien bears with me, indeed I don't!'

Paula smiled. 'He probably appreciates that all artists are allowed their idiosyncrasies, and so he is patient with yours. And anyway, what of them? You have a right to be yourself.'

Louise nodded gloomily. 'Perhaps. *If* I were an artist——' Returning to the matter of their search, she spread her hands emptily. 'Well, there it is. I seem to have lost or destroyed the sketch, though if it should turn up, you shall have it.' She added hesitantly, 'I should tell you—that is, Gratien suggested that now you are one of us we might call you by your first name instead of always "Miss Raymond". Would you mind?'

'Of course not. I'd be very glad if you would,' said Paula, pleased that the suggestion had come from Gratien, and looking forward to the accented sound her name would make on his lips. She was to be slightly less gratified—as she suspected Monique intended she should be—when Monique, hearing Louise address her as Paula for the first time, commented, 'Well, of course, you are just staff, aren't you—like Emilie and Berthe, and people don't usually call their cooks Madame or Mademoiselle, do they?'

To which Paula, becoming used now to Monique's petty resentment of her, replied evenly, 'That's so, I expect. I am being put in my place.'

She did most of her shopping for the table in Libourne, but it was to St Emilion that she went for pleasure, often choosing to walk there through the lanes and come back by the country bus which stuttered its noisy way from hamlet to hamlet, tossing out packets of newspapers, picking up crates of chickens, carrying verbal messages for its passengers to their aunts or mothers or cousins and having its time-schedule ignored by its driver, who was apt to move off from the terminus as soon as his bus was full.

Rich as St Emilion was in historic sights and monuments, Paula preferred to spend these afternoons strolling its narrow streets or sitting under its plane-trees on its market square, watching the old men play *boules* on the sunbaked earth, and the old women gossiping at their doors, the rest of the town's populace being singularly thin on the ground, since almost all the able-bodied residents, from schoolchildren to mothers of families, were at work in the vineyards, competing with the too-swiftly passing time of harvest.

It was while she was enjoying this lazy vigil one afternoon that Paula became aware of the interested glances of a young man who, after parking his car, passed in front of her once, walked on a little way, came back, and chose a bench at an angle to hers a short way off, so that he hadn't to turn to watch her.

And watch her he did, as she knew very well without having to look at him. It was the gaze of a male with time on his hands and opportunism in view; she had only to glance his way with even cool interest and he would regard himself as invited.

She was wrong. He didn't wait for an invitation, but presently moved over to stand in front of her, smiling experimentally. His figure was loosely-knit and he was handsome in a conventional way; dark moustache, small pointed beard, dimpled chin; too confident of radiating a charm which she found it easy to resist. He said, 'Pretty quiet around here, when everyone is at the grape-gathering. Aren't you lonely?'

She said, 'It is quiet. But I rather like the town when it is as quiet as this.'

'Not lonely? But you are alone? May I sit?'

She was tempted to the slick reply of 'Why not? it's a public seat,' but thought silence more meaningful. He sat down, easing his slacks over his knees and

73

crossing his legs as if prepared to stay. He offered cigarettes which she refused and glanced at her watch, to see how soon she could leave to catch the bus. She could get up and walk away now, of course, but hadn't quite the nerve to administer such a direct snub.

He had tilted his head, as if listening. 'Your accent—you aren't French, mademoiselle?'

'No, I'm English.'

Gallantly surprised, '*No*? But your French is perfect! Are you on holiday here?'

'No. Are you?' She hadn't meant to show the interest of the question, but it broke up the succession of 'No's'.

He said, 'You might say I'm on a busman's holiday. I'm in public relations for a firm of shippers, and I'm staying at the Château Aragon with——'

'At the Château Aragon?'

'Yes. Comte Montdoret's place. Why, do you know it?'

'I know of it. It's not far from where I am myself.'

'Really? And that is——?' he pressed.

'The Château de Tourcy.' Lest he should suppose she was a guest, she added, 'I'm acting as caterer there for the weeks of the vintage.'

'Really?' he said again. 'With Gratien and Louise de Tourcy? Of course I know them. I've been to these parts before. So you lay on all the gourmet meals for their visiting firemen?' He looked her over boldly. 'No one ever told me that professional cooks could come in such attractive packages!'

Paula looked at her watch again and stood up.

'I'm afraid I must go. I have a bus to catch at the terminus,' she said.

He stood beside her. 'Let me drive you there.'

'No, I can walk.'

'But my car is just there.' He pointed to it, and held out his hand. 'My name is Guy Crespigny. And you are—Madame? Mademoiselle? Miss——?'

'Raymond, Paula Raymond,' she supplied reluctantly.

'And so, names exchanged as in the most correct of introductions, you will allow me to drive you to the terminus?'

She accepted. It wasn't far and she could part from him there.

On the way he asked, 'You came over by bus from de Tourcy?'

'No, I walked in. I do sometimes, when I have time to spare.'

'And I suppose you've done all the tourist things?' They were passing St Emilion's Hermitage at the time. 'There, for instance? You'll have queued up with the local girls and offered the Saint your two pins?'

'Yes, I've done that.'

'With what result, if he knew what he was about? Though as if one need ask! You are sure to be already engaged?'

She left that as a statement, not a question, and prepared to say goodbye to him as they reached the terminal. But although the bus should have been in and ready to move off in five minutes, its parking slot was empty and no passengers were waiting. Her companion alighted from his car and went with her

75

as she approached a man in an inspector's cap, sitting on a low wall.

'The seventeen-twenty bus that runs through to Libourne by the river road—where is it?' she asked him.

He chewed on his cigarette. 'Already gone, madame,' he said.

'But'—she tapped the glass of her watch—'it's barely seventeen-fifteen!'

He conceded that. 'True, madame. But the bus had its full complement of passengers and baggage, so it left.'

'Before time? But it had no right to do that!'

A Gallic shrug. 'If it could take no more passengers, why should it wait?'

'At least to tell them so, I should have thought,' Paula said in exasperation. 'And that's the last bus, isn't it, this evening?'

'For Libourne by that route, alas yes, madame.'

As she turned away, Guy Crespigny's hand was urgently at her elbow. 'Why worry?' he said. 'No problem at all. I'll drive you back to de Tourcy on my way back to Aragon. I was only out on an idle drive around, and my time is my own.'

She had no choice, short of walking back, for which she hadn't bargained. She thanked him and got back into the car. After all, he claimed acquaintanceship with the de Tourcys, and he was staying on business at Aragon, which made him not quite the importunate wolf he had seemed at first.

She asked him if he were weekending at Aragon, but he said No. He was on a fairly open-ended invitation. His firm dealt extensively in Château

Aragon wines, and he was engaged in preparing a new catalogue. 'I shall certainly be here for the Vendanges Ball the Montdorets give. Are you going to it?'

It was the first Paula had heard of it, and she said so, finding it unnecessary to point out that as mere 'staff', she would hardly expect an invitation. She added that she supposed there was no doubt that Monsieur and Mademoiselle de Tourcy and their young protégés would be there.

Guy Crespigny agreed with a knowing nod. 'No doubt at all that Gratien de Tourcy will be there. Pretty little La Courtet will see to that for sure!' he said, confirming Paula's conviction that she could take both his sly innuendoes and his foreseeable gallantries in only very small doses.

He drove up to the front of the château just as Gratien came out of the main doorway. Gratien stopped, looked from Paula to her companion as they alighted, and addressed him with a slight frown. 'You are—er—Crespigny, aren't you? You are staying at Aragon?'

'Yes, just arrived. And happily, just in time to play knight errant to Mademoiselle Raymond who had missed her bus, or rather, whose bus had chosen to miss *her*!'

'Really? Where was this?' Gratien asked Paula.

'In St Emilion. The bus had left too early, and Monsieur Crespigny kindly——'

'If you use that bus much, you should know it is apt to do that, and you should make allowances,' he cut in.

'Which I certainly shall in future,' she retorted

with warmth, annoyed by his tone of censure, however mild, and Guy Crespigny begged in mock horror, 'Oh, don't tell her that, or she mightn't let me rescue her next time she appears to be in distress! She might give me the cold shoulder and tell me she had "made allowances",' a plea which fell so flat with the other two that, with a shrug, and a word of farewell, he got into his car and drove off.

Gratien said, 'You know, I thought you understood that you have the use of the runabout when you go out alone? Why weren't you using it today?'

'Because I wasn't shopping in St Emilion. I had walked over because I needed the exercise, and I enjoy travelling by the bus too.'

'So how did you meet Crespigny? Did he happen to be at the bus stop when you found the bus had gone?'

Paula wondered whether he knew the extent to which his questions implied rebuke, and decided on nonchalance as the best retort.

'No. In fact, he had picked me up earlier—spoken to me while I was sitting on the Square, and when I said I must go to catch the bus, he offered to drive me to the terminus,' she said.

'Spoke to you—just like that?'

She smiled faintly. 'Men do do it sometimes, you know—if they think a girl is alone.'

'*And*, I suppose, if they decide that the girl in question looks—easy?' Gratien demanded on a savage note which made almost an insult of 'easy'. But Paula refused to be roused by it. She said, 'Oh, come, you must know that some men will chance their arm with any girl. They are brash enough to risk the snub which they may, or may not, get.'

'Which Crespigny didn't get from you?'

'There seemed no point,' she explained patiently. 'He was there; I was; both of us obviously at leisure, and I knew—or thought I did—that I could leave him as soon as I had got to the bus. After all, you can't just slap the face of a man, merely to stand on your dignity. Besides, he's staying with the Comte and Comtesse Montdoret, and told me he knew you.'

'He couldn't have made that his introduction to you. He spoke to you first?'

'But I've told you he did! Look'—she conceded —'I'll admit that it was as blatant a pick-up as I've ever experienced, but——'

'And you've had experience of all kinds?'

'What woman hasn't?' she retorted airily. 'One learns to play it by ear. But as I was saying, in this case he wasn't without background, and neither was I, which established a bit of rapport—no more and no less, in fact, than if we'd been properly introduced. So I'm afraid I don't understand your criticism of me for being reasonably pleasant with him and letting him see me safely back. Unless, that is, you know something about the man which you haven't told me.'

'Something to his detriment?' Gratien shook his head. 'No.'

'Well then——?' she appealed emptily.

'I still don't have to care for what I've seen of him to date,' Gratien said as he turned and left her.

The next weekend's visitors were all French journalists, doing their annual rounds of the châteaux, assessing the merits of the year's harvest for the benefit of their columns in the press. The following weekend party was to be a socially mixed affair of the de Tourcys' friends, some shipping brokers and some hoteliers from the Riviera. It was in the lull between these two that Gratien took up his promise to instruct Paula in wine craft, sending her first to his culture manager in the vineyards while the gathering was in full swing; each vine, each row, being methodically denuded by the busy secateurs; each *douil* filled to its capacity of the quantity of grapes enough to fill a giant cask of raw wine; each *douil*-loaded lorry rolling away to serve the greedy maw of the *égrappoirs* of the processing plant in the first stage of the grape's long conversion into wine.

The culture manager took time to sketch in for her the wine's story to that point—its preference for a light mixed soil, for the sun and rain and wind of a gentle climate, its frailty in the face of hail or frost, its sturdy resistance to occasional snow.

In the region the vines were kept short, no more than waist-high, in strictly ordered rows, with scarcely a leaf or a tendril that wasn't playing its part in the design.

'And do you know who, it's said, taught us how to prune?' the manager asked. 'Donkeys, if you please! Donkeys!'

Paula echoed, 'Donkeys? How?'

'It's an old story—true or not, one can't know. It was in the days when the monasteries owned most of the region's land; grew grapes on it, as we do, and used panniered donkeys and mules to carry the crop. They let the vines run riot and didn't know why they deteriorated until one winter the donkeys on one vineyard got loose, ate them down to ground level and——'

'And didn't kill them?' Paula laughed.

'Kill them? Far from it. That yard had a better crop than ever the next season, and the story got around. And as you see, we've pruned hard ever since.' He broke off to lay a guarding hand on Paula's arm as a heavily-laden lorry lumbered towards them on the uneven, rutted ground. 'Take care, mademoiselle' he warned. 'These trucks have poor balance when they are loaded; always give them way.'

He went with her to the *chai*, the main winestore where all the later action was, and where, to Paula's surprise, Gratien met them and said he would take over.

He showed her the *douils* having their loads guided into the *égrappoirs*, the stalks and pips emerging from one vent, and the slightly crushed grapes and the skins being pumped into the first fermentation vats, where the resultant pulp under its thick 'hat' of skins would turn its natural sugars into alcohol in a matter of seven to twelve days. At this stage the 'hat' would be removed and pressed before being re-added to the fermented juices. 'To give colour to the red wine,' Gratien explained. 'We don't process the skins at all for white.'

The second and more gentle fermentation at lesser heat would take place after the wine was transferred to its first cask, he said. There it would begin to develop its bouquet, lose its acids and leave its lees behind when it was pumped into fresh casks every three to four months of its maturing, which would take at least eighteen months and possibly more, and continued in the bottle to 'round off its corners', Gratien quoted the local saying. The de Tourcy wine which was now going out proudly labelled with the de Tourcy coat-of-arms and the Bordeaux stamp of quality was of a not later vintage than two seasons ago—its full cycle of grape to shipped bottle complete.

As they came out on to the rough road leading past the *chai* Paula asked what made the Bordeaux region so famed for its wine—why there, rather than anywhere else?

Gratien said, 'Soil, drainage by pebbles washed down from the mountains, a less than sub-tropical climate, vines neither too young nor too old, the right varieties for the soil, the ideal number to the hectare, drastic pruning and centuries of know-how behind us.'

'That's quite a list. Do you——?'

But the question died on her tongue as she saw she hadn't Gratien's attention and why. He was looking back over his shoulder, his stance rigid, his tawny eyes alight with anger, as one of the *douil* lorries came rocking and lurching at a furious pace down the slope towards them. Behind the driver's cab on the floor of the lorry four *douils* piled high with grapes skated and shunted, and as Gratien muttered, 'The fool!' and then to Paula, 'Wait. I must see who this lunatic is,' the vehicle swerved madly and one of them crashed through the side slats and hurled its massive weight straight into the watchers' path.

There was an instant when Paula knew it must knock her down; another—when she knew she had escaped its menace, thanks to Gratien's arms wrapped close about her body; another still, when he almost flung her from him, and standing square himself to the bounding great vessel, stopped it by sheer brute strength.

He looked round for her and came to her where, thrown off balance by the violence of his action, she was on her knees on the *pavé*.

He helped her up by taking both her hands, and for a moment they stood close, breast to breast, while she steadied. They were both panting as he said, 'I'm sorry, but that was necessary. Are you all right?' and she answered, 'Y—yes', and, 'I know.'

Meanwhile, as the lorry had careered on, a second *douil* had slithered through the breach made by the first, bounced hard once and rolled away on its side. Grapes were scattered everywhere; the noise had brought a crowd of workers to the doors of the *chai*, and when the lorry finally came to a tipsy halt, Gratien was there awaiting it, his face thunderous.

The driver climbed down from the cab and faced him. 'So?' Gratien demanded of a sulky-faced Milon, trying to look nonchalant and not succeeding, 'so perhaps you'll explain yourself, my friend? And your explanation had better be good.'

'I was bored,' Milon muttered. 'There's nothing to do around here. I asked one of the drivers to let me have a go, and how was I to know that when it had a load up, the thing was going to handle like a bucking steer?'

'"It wasn't my fault. Nobody told me",' Gratien sneered.

'Well, nobody did.'

'And should you need telling that a lorry of that size on the vineyard tracks and this *pavé* isn't going to handle as easily as a baby carriage? Anyway, why the speed? Showing off? To whom?'

'That—happened. Before the sway started, I had put on a bit of speed, and when the load began to shift, I couldn't control it. I had to let it race down the slope and bank on being able to brake once I got on the level.'

'That's your story. You saw Paula and me ahead of you?'

'Yes. But you weren't in any danger. The racket alone would make you get out of the way.'

'Of the lorry, yes. But not of what did happen. Do you realise that if that first *douil* had struck Paula, she might have been killed?'

To that Milon said nothing, and Gratien went on, 'Meanwhile, as consolation for her not having been killed or injured on my estate by an accident which needn't have happened, perhaps I'm to be congratulated that all you've succeeded in is to destroy the makings of around half a *tonneau* of wine?'

'I've told you—I couldn't help it,' Milon growled. He looked about him at the mess of grape-pulp and splintered wood. 'I suppose you'd like me to clear it up?'

'Well, it would help,' Gratien said, his tone

falsely bland as he turned away, his gesture inviting Paula to go with him.

She went, hoping she would never find herself in any situation such as had evoked from him as caustic an anger as he had vented on Milon. Her legs were still shaking as she re-lived the moment of that great weight-laden tub bowling and crashing towards her; and the next, when Gratien had swept her into his arms.

His protective reflex had been instinctive; he would have done the same for anyone in the danger he foresaw; snatched at them as urgently; guarded them as closely. But the moment of an embrace which had been thrust upon him had been exciting for her; had set her pulse racing, and no longer in fear. She had time to think now that, had they both willed it in love and at a common impulse, the experience of their nearness, her yielding to the taut strength of his hold, the pounding of their hearts would have been little different. Except that it would have lasted, been repeated—as that moment's experience would not. It had no past behind it and no future ahead.

CHAPTER FIVE

It was a day or two later that Guy Crespigny and Solange Courtet drove from Aragon, uninvited but warmly welcomed by Louise.

When they arrived, Paula, who had been consulting Louise about menus, excused herself fairly quickly and returned to the kitchen, carrying with her a message to Emilie to serve coffee and *petits fours* for the guests. Paula herself was checking the stores she would need for the weekend when Guy Crespigny strolled in and was there ready for a neat fielding of a can of chestnut purée when it tottered and rolled from a shelf.

'Oh——' Paula took the can from him when he proffered it with an exaggerated bow. 'I didn't know you were there.'

'No? I asked permission of Louise to come and see where all the action is.' He looked about him. 'This is your kingdom? The demesne where you hold sway?'

'Only temporarily, and then only in partnership with Emilie the cook, its permanent ruler,' she told him.

'Two of you? I thought it was a universally accepted axiom that a couple of women can never share a kitchen amicably?' he mocked.

'I'd say it depends on the women,' Paula said drily. 'Emilie and I seem to manage quite happily.'

'Good for you.' As Paula closed the louvred door of a cupboard and moved over to the central table, he strolled about, affecting an interest in the kitchen's appointments which did not deceive Paula. She suspected he had come to see her, and so he confirmed when he came to sit, straddle-legged, on a chair at her side.

'When will you be going to St E. again?' he asked.

'I don't know. Not this week, certainly,' she said.

'But elsewhere? Somewhere? Somewhere where you would let me drive you? Give you luncheon? Take you out to dinner?'

'Thank you, but I'm afraid not. It's Thursday now, and I shall be busy all through the weekend.'

'But you do have time of your own?' he persisted.

'Of course.'

'Then why not spend some of it with me? Or when I want to see you, must I always play escort to Solange Courtet who no doubt has her own good reasons for descending on Louise and Gratien? Not that one has to tire one's brain, guessing what they are. Besides, pots and pans aren't the most romantic of settings, are they? Believe me, I could do far better by moonlight!'

'Could you?' Paula hoped her tone was cold enough to snub, but undaunted, 'Try me and see!' Guy retorted archly, and she was only saved from further clichés of flirtation by Emilie's return, when, with a shrug of resignation, he took himself off, much to Paula's relief. She didn't find him attractive, and she had no intention of indulging a below-stairs affair with one of the de Tourcys' intimates, and particularly not with this one, against whom Gratien hadn't troubled to hide his prejudice.

But she was to find Guy wasn't so easily headed off. When he accompanied Solange, who came often, though he didn't again seek out Paula in the kitchen, whenever they met he contrived to delay her, and she was so often invited to join the château party for morning coffee when he was there that she suspected him of engineering her summons by Louise. Sometimes she was able to plead that she was too busy; sometimes she had no excuse for refusing and had to suffer his all-too-obvious gallantries under the eye of everyone else who was present. Having struck up a friendship with Milon, he was even there when Solange was not, and it was at one such session, when the two had left together to go swimming, that Louise produced to Paula a letter addressed to her by the Comtesse Montdoret, hand-delivered, Louise said, by Guy Crespigny.

Paula opened it. It was a formal invitation to her to the Vendange Ball at Aragon; third-person worded, though below it Clara Montdoret had added a friendly, 'Please come', and signed it C. M.

As Paula looked up from it Louise asked anxiously, 'You will accept? In a note to me Clara said she would so like you to, and it is such an event of our season that I don't think you should refuse.'

'Refuse what?' Gratien put the question as he came on to the patio where they were sitting, and Louise told him, 'Clara's invitation to Paula to come with us to their Ball.'

'But of course she can't refuse,' ruled Gratien,

88

making an order of it. 'Was she——?' he turned to Paula—'Were you thinking of refusing, then?'

'No—that is, I've only just been invited, and I haven't had time to think.'

'Then take time. As much as you like, so long as you accept. I'd taken it for granted that Paula would be one of our party'—he was speaking to Louise now—'and I'd supposed that Clara would assume it too?'

'Yes, well, perhaps she didn't think it was clear she expected Paula. So she sent a separate invitation to her by Guy Crespigny, and I'd only just handed it to her,' Louise explained.

'*Brought* by Guy Crespigny, and *inspired* by Guy Crespigny, no doubt.' From the chaise-longue on which she lay, Monique's small murmur was barely audible, but Gratien heard it.

'What do you mean by that?' he asked.

Monique shrugged. 'Nothing, except that Guy doesn't hide the fact that it is Paula he comes to see. And that it seems funny the Comtesse didn't include Paula when she invited the rest of us to her Ball.'

'But, Monique dear,' put in Louise, 'Clara Montdoret never does ask us formally. She concludes that we know she expects us, and we always go. In fact, I don't think she has mentioned the Ball at all since before you and Milon and Paula came.'

'Oh, very well. I'm sorry I spoke,' said Monique testily. Gratien said nothing, and if he hadn't questioned Monique's remark so sharply Paula could have hoped he hadn't noticed the linking of her name with Guy Crespigny's. But since he had, she suspected he shared Monique's idea that it had been Guy who had persuaded his hostess to invite her. Whether or no, in all reason it was no business of Gratien's. But the thought made Paula writhe all the same.

The weather held. The season promised to be a good one. The *douils* were filled; disgorged their loads into the maw of the *égrappoirs*; the red-purple pulp flowed into vats; was processed at the right temperature to turn its sugars into alcohol; regained its discarded 'hat' for its richer colouring and was pumped into its first casks to begin a career of change and clearing and tasting which would not end until long after Paula's time in the region was over.

While everyone else on the estate could follow it through the seasons of its maturing, she could only see the conclusion of the story of earlier vintages —in the ordered bustle of the dressing and packing stores which continued year-round as the filled bottles, 'dressed' in their château labels and foil caps, went out in château-branded crates to grace the tables of the world. Once, watching the skill and care of the women engaged on this last service— their almost reverential respect for the wine—Paula remembered how Gratien had said that on a corrupt vineyard it was probably at this stage that fraud could most easily take place. There had never been any risk of it in de Tourcy, he had claimed, and it would be remarkable if there ever were, Paula thought, considering the loving policing of the precious cargoes in the dressing stores. Mothers putting their children to bed could scarcely have appeared more dedicated than these dressers were!

On the vineyards Gratien shared a large office and staff with his manager, but in his private office in the château he had a library of books on wine, of which he had made Paula free, if she cared to borrow any of them. She had gladly accepted, by-passing the technical manuals on the shelves in favour of the many others which told and illustrated the romance and history of the craft.

The story was an age-old one of land cherished and guarded; of family; of noble houses; of fiercely loyal people, and sometimes of land, abandoned to dereliction through misfortune or squandered profits or death, but restored again to health and production through someone's hard work and faith that it must not die.

Father and son and sometimes daughter, and their children in their own turn, inheriting and marching with the times in some things, in others yielding nothing to modernity when the old ways were better—it was a tradition which Paula longed to share; to feel that kind of past behind her, and the future hers.

It was on the day before the Ball at Aragon that she went to return a volume of engravings of some of the present-day châteaux as they had appeared in the seventeenth and eighteenth centuries. Gratien was not there, so she replaced the book, then glanced through the shelves in search of another one he had recommended to her.

She found it, but in pulling it out, displaced another which fell to the floor, open and face downwards. 'Careless!' she blamed herself, and stooped to it. It was a well-used treatise on the chemistry of wine, full of graphs and formulae which meant nothing to her, but from between its pages a loose sheet had fluttered—a square of drawing paper creased once across for its insertion in the book, but fanning open now to show a pencil sketch she had seen before—Louise's original rough of Paula herself in the château kitchen, the sketch which Louise had wanted to give her, but had lost instead!

Paula stared at it wonderingly. How had it found its way to this hiding-place? Only, certainly, by the hand of someone who had put it there—why? For tidiness, having found it lying about? Or for safe keeping? And whose hand? Logically, Gratien's, since the book was his, but surely impossibly Gratien's, since he could have no reason for treasuring a memento of her? He must have picked it up by mistake in Louise's studio and later forgotten it. Paula couldn't remember whether Louise ever mentioned its loss in his hearing. But of course she couldn't have, or it wouldn't still be here. She would have reclaimed it, wanting to give it to Paula. No, its loss and its finding must have slipped both their memories, Paula decided, longing though not daring to hope that Gratien had helped himself to it because he liked it and had wanted it enough to put it away here where only he knew its whereabouts.

It was tantalizing, not knowing. But the doubt and the distance between them forbade her questioning his reasons, and by the same token she was reluctant to admit to Louise that she knew where it was. Puzzled, wishing ... she put it back between the pages and restored the book to the shelf.

For the Ball she wore the most formal gown she had —a narrowly-cut sheath of green velvet, the hem draping to a small fishtail train and its throat-high neckline cut away to a deep V at the back. There was nothing she could do with her short hair-style but burnish its highlights and curve its ends forward on her cheeks. She carried a silver brocade envelope-bag and wore no jewellery; without knowing Gratien's preferences in women's clothes, she dressed for his approval as she would have done to please a lover whose taste she knew, who would praise her choice and claim he thought her beautiful. The silly, impossible dream!

Monique wore russet red—none too happy a choice with her sallow colouring. Louise's large-patterned dress was fussy, with fringes and an accompanying shawl which frequently slipped from her narrow shoulders and needed to be anchored by her close-held elbows. Paula had yearned to unpin those earphones of hair and coil it instead into a soft chignon, but she hadn't liked to suggest it, and Louise was happily unconscious that her hair-style was decades out of date.

Monique was happy in assuming that Gratien went as her escort; Paula was welcome to Milon and Louise didn't expect one. In any case there was room for them all in his big car, and Monique saw to it that she sat beside him, ousting Louise, whose place it should surely have been.

For the occasion the Château Aragon was floodlit, and Paula thought she had never seen a building which took on so much enchantment.

The Château was one of the truly 'great houses' of the region, its entrance through wide wrought-iron gates leading to a drive between formal beds massed with flowers below a stone-balustrade terrace reached by a wide flight of stone steps. Massive pillars formed the portico to a mansion in the style of a palace of the sixteenth century, which was in fact its date. Under the floodlamps it had an ethereal appearance: Cinderella might have danced there and escaped down these very steps to disappear in the shadows of these gardens. Solid as its structure really was, by this light it looked not quite of this world—an elegant stage set which, when it had served its purpose, might find itself dismantled and packed away.

The main guest rooms consisted of two long salons—the Blue Room where people would dance, and behind it a Summer Salon, one side of which was open on this warm autumn night to another terrace, discreetly dark in contrast with the light and colour of the guest rooms—an open-air place for 'sitting out'.

It seemed to Paula that everyone seemed to know everyone else, but they were friendly and outgoing to her, the stranger. Almost as soon as an introduction was flung at her, she would be claimed for dancing by the newcomer, who in due course would pass her on to another partner with another careless introduction, which she would take in momentarily and promptly forget. It didn't matter. Dancing was the thing. The Comte and Comtesse had guests who were French, English, Dutch, German, Swiss, and before the evening was half over Paula felt she must have met a cross-section of them all. To those who took an interest in who and what she was, she took an impish delight in telling, 'I'm an English cook' and watching their surprise—none of it patronising, but almost always there.

'As if,' she joked to Louise, 'they could accept my being English, and also that I was a cook. But as if, in these gastronomic parts, an *English* cook was a creature beyond their ken!'

Early on she had looked out for Solange Courtet, a top-of-the-Christmas-tree fairy doll, inevitably in white; had seen her claim Gratien from Monique; had seen him dancing with her—tiny, exquisite, needing to laugh up at him from well below his shoulder.

He danced with Monique too, and with Paula herself; once crossing the room to claim her, once accidentally at the distance of a modern approach-and-retreat affair, where no one was anyone's partner in particular. They had both moved on, quickly lost to each other in the cavorting, gesticulating crowd.

It had not been far into the evening when Guy Crespigny had sought her out, complimenting her on her looks and claiming—which she didn't want to believe—that it had been at his suggestion that the Comtesse had invited her. Even if it were true, she resented his assumption that it put her in debt to him, owing him as much of her company as he wished to claim. Whenever she found herself standing alone, he was there at her side, a possessive hand beneath her elbow asserting its rights.

Once, to escape him, she retired to the cloakroom and was using her lipstick before a mirror when she became aware of two dowagers who, finding themselves at adjacent mirrors, were deep in cosy chat.

'They make an attractive couple, and on both sides it would be an advantageous match,' said one.

'Yes, indeed. One understands that it began as a romance of their schooldays——'

'Of their schooldays?' The first speaker shook her head. 'Hardly possible, that, I think. When Gratien was in his teens, Solange Courtet would scarcely be out of the nursery, surely?'

The other lady waved the objection aside. 'Merely a figure of speech. What I meant was that they have met here every year since Solange was a schoolgirl—at an age when she first needed a hero to worship and found Gratien not unwilling to accept her homage. Like any young man, he would have had his conceits, and now that she is grown-up and the difference in their ages has smoothed out—Well, it is a match I would approve for *my* daughter if I had one, I must say.'

'Or for your son?'

A laugh and a shrug. 'Oh, come, Madame Moisier, you must know that in these days a son does not look for one's approval of his choice—he presents her to his parents as a *fait accompli*!' And the rueful laugh being echoed by the other lady, each gave a final pat to her elegant head, picked up her bag, and they rustled away.

Of course it was no more than Paula could have guessed for herself. The French thought so much

96

in terms of suitable 'matches'; even Gratien probably wasn't blind to the advantages of an alliance
with the heiress to a great wine-shipping concern,
nor Solange ignorant of the dignity of becoming
Gratien's young bride and châtelaine of de Tourcy.
And add to that—Paula winced at the thought—
add to that this long tradition of their friendship
and attraction to each other, and what more likely,
after all?

Louise had defended it. Monique, jealous of it,
feared it. Paula recognised it as an affair with a
future she did not want to be there to see.

She went to supper in a party which included
Monique and some German boys, one of whom was
so anxious to practise English with her that she was
able to use him as bulwark between herself and Guy
Crespigny during several dances. She had no German, but they communicated in a mixture of French
and English, and for the space of at least half an
hour they sat out on the patio while he struggled
earnestly with idioms and constructions which were
new to him. They were on their way back to the
dance-floor when Paula felt the inevitable touch on
her elbow and inwardly recoiled. But it was not
Guy Crespigny; it was Gratien.

'Are you free for the next dance?' he asked.

'Yes, I think so.'

'Then may I?'

Paula glanced at her companion, who bowed formally. 'Thank you. I have taken too much of your
time,' he said, and effaced himself in the crowd.

Face to face with Paula, moving easily to the slow
rhythm of the freestyle dance, Gratien said,

'You've been off the floor for a long time. Were you sitting out?'

She nodded and smiled. 'And giving an English lesson.'

'To your late partner? I don't know him. Who is he?'

'His name is Karl Richter. He already speaks English very well, but he evidently believes in making the most of his opportunities.'

As soon as she spoke she realised the double meaning which might be read into that and was relieved when Gratien laughed.

'The opportunity *only* of perfecting his English?' he queried.

'*Only* of perfecting his English,' she replied demurely, and saw that he believed her. Guy Crespigny, she reflected, would have made coy capital of the opening she had given him and would have worked the innuendo to death.

She wondered how many duty dances Gratien felt he owed her—the one they had already had and this one? But when the music stopped, he turned again towards the terrace. 'A drink outside?' he invited. 'What will you have?'

She told him, and while he went to the bar she strolled out, going over to the stone balustrade to lean on it, looking out over the park. He joined her there, lifted his glass to her and they drank. They were not alone, for though the late night was cooling, a few other people who had escaped the noise and crowds of the house still lingered, tête-à-tête or in small groups.

Their nearest neighbours were a couple some distance away, mere shadows at the stone coping, seen only in head and shoulders silhouette. A man and a girl like themselves, but there was intimacy in their closeness and in the laughter which punctuated the murmur of their talk. Paula glanced at them and quickly away, envying them a little. She thought Gratien might not have noticed them at all until the girl's laugh rang out more loudly, a long ripple of sound on a teasing, provocative note. Then Gratien glanced that way and back again.

'We are eavesdropping. That's Solange,' he said.

'Yes.' There had been no mistaking that bubbling laugh. Paula straightened, prepared to move away, but Gratien did not stir.

'Enjoying herself at her partner's expense—the poor wretch. She learnt coquetry in her cradle, and she chooses her victims with flair.' He sipped his drink calmly.

Paula pondered this curiously frank comment in silence. Didn't he mind Solange's flirtatious exchanges with other men? Or was it rather, as people said, that he knew her so well and was so sure of her himself that he could afford to be tolerant of how she used her charm? Paula knew she would prefer that he didn't mind.

Meanwhile Solange and her companion were indulging some physical skirmishing. She stepped back, laughing and waving provocatively some small object she held in her hand.

'Come and get it!' she taunted him, her raised voice distinct now. 'You'll need to use force, but I dare you——!' Still laughing, she stepped back another pace, well out of his reach if at that moment

99

he had not suddenly plunged for her, caught her as she turned to run, reached to take from her up-raised hand whatever it was they were disputing, then turned her into his arms and kissed her with deliberation on her lips.

She giggled excitedly, made a feint of slapping his face before she ducked from his hold and ran, her filmy white skirts frothing round her. She looked back once to see if he were following her. He wasn't. He was strolling nonchalantly, as if, as far as he was concerned, the game was over. As he had plunged from the shadow cast by the balustrade, Paula knew that Gratien must have recognised him, as she had. He was Guy Crespigny.

Gratien said dryly, 'H'm. Seems I was wrong. No hypnotized rabbit, he. More of a case of "Greek meets Greek".'

'What do you mean by that?'

'Surely? When a practised philanderer tries con-clusions with an equally experienced coquette, it's anyone's war to win.'

Paula couldn't quite take that. She carried no brief for Crespigny, but 'philanderer' sounded like sheer prejudice.

'Isn't that rather sweeping?' she asked. 'At worst, it could amount to slander.'

Gratien shook his head. 'Not of Solange, who has made a fine art of her scalp-hunting. Nor of Cres-pigny, who boasts of his conquests and, if encour-aged, is always ready to furnish names and details.'

'Is that why you warned me against him when I let him drive me back from St Emilion? But you said then you didn't know anything to his detriment,' Paula reminded him.

'I didn't then. I do now. So may we leave it at that?' His tone held finality, and she agreed, 'Of course,' though she longed to know whether Guy Crespigny had bragged of her as one of his conquests, and if so, whether Gratien had believed him.

There was silence until Gratien asked her impressions of Aragon, and she found herself relating rather shyly her whimsy about Cinderella and the fairyland unreality of the château's façade.

'To me, under the floodlights, it looked as if it didn't quite exist, and I couldn't be surprised if it weren't there tomorrow morning. Silly, I know——' her voice trailed away.

'And none too accurate on facts,' Gratien commented. 'I thought it was Cinderella herself who lost her new identity and found herself back in her kitchen the next morning?' He paused on a short laugh. 'Aren't we repeating ourselves? Isn't this where we came in?'

She turned to look at him. 'What do you mean—came in?'

'On the odd temporary effects of transformation, don't you remember? Nurses in and out of uniform, women dentists, cooks——?'

Remembering, 'Oh—yes,' Paula agreed.

'Just so. On the value to a woman adopting a different image occasionally, for getting herself noticed and admired and courted, as Cinderella was when she sloughed her everyday gear for an elegance she carried excitingly.'

'Admired and courted for just one night! And where did that get her? On your own showing—back in her kitchen the next day!' retorted Paula, taking her cue with spirit.

'But she had left a lot of curiosity behind her. Enough——'

For some minutes now her inner woman's sense had known she was aiding and abetting a fantasy that he intended should lead somewhere personal to them both. The look he had given her in his pause, implicit with admiration, confirmed it and tempted her to the reckless, provocative question, 'Enough for what?'

'Enough for her to have made her challenge felt; to have intrigued people with her "infinite variety", wouldn't you say?'

'She still went back to her kitchen.'

'Perhaps. Anyway, nobody can live more than one night at a time.' He was not looking at her now, but was watching the uncontrolled tremble of her fingers on the stem of her empty glass. He had already put his own aside and now took hers from her as he went on, 'What's more, you know very well that we're not talking about Cinderella's night out, but this one——'

And as she knew they would, and as in the headiness of her mood she had neither the will nor the power to stop them, his arms went round her and drew her close. Though she knew he meant to, he did not kiss her at once, but held her off, his eyes travelling over her from head to foot; his scrutiny, she thought, that of a connoisseur, when she longed for it to be a lover's. And when his lips did seek her mouth it was with expert deliberation, stilling the wild pulse of her craving to respond.

She broke from him. 'Wh—what was that?' she stammered, one hand to a flaming cheek.

'You could take it as a tribute, if nothing more,' he said.

'I—see. A tribute to a chameleon act which you felt you ought to reward?' she scorned.

'If you feel rewarded, yes.'

'I don't particularly.'

'You'd rather I'd thought up some prettily worded compliment on your looks tonight—of which I daresay you've already received several?'

She flushed, recalling Guy Crespigny's trite flattery at sight of her on her arrival. 'If I have, they weren't in such cavalier terms as yours,' she said.

'No? Then at least I've been original.'

'Not to mention presumptuous——'

'For paying my homage in my own way to an expert cook turned equally polished *mondaine* for one evening? Is this where I apologise for my indiscretion?'

'You needn't, as long as you admit it was an indiscretion.'

'If you saw it so, then we're agreed,' he said carelessly, destroying a dream.

CHAPTER SIX

BACK in the ballroom Paula hoped that, whether or not he knew she had seen him with Solange, Guy Crespigny would have the grace to leave her alone, and he did. Not so Solange, who made a point of joining her when she saw Paula sitting by herself.

Spreading her skirts demurely and linking her fingers in her lap, Solange said with the air of a penitent child, 'I expect you are very cross with me, aren't you? But it was all for Gratien's benefit really. It just happened to be Guy who was handy, that was all.'

Cryptic as this sounded, Paula partly understood it. 'Why apologise to me?' she asked. 'If you are talking about that piece of byplay on the terrace just now, Guy Crespigny is a free agent, and so are you.'

The baby-blue eyes widened. 'But he is your property, your beau! We both knew you saw us, and I meant Gratien to. But I was sorry you had to—it was just bad timing, that was all. It didn't *mean* anything, you understand. You don't need to be jealous.'

Paula said, 'I'm not jealous. Guy isn't a property I particularly want.'

'He wants *you*—or he says he does.'

'Then if he means that, I'm surprised that he

lent himself to that bit of nonsense with you, which you say was planned.'

Solange nodded. 'That's right. To impress Gratien.'

'To impress him with what?'

'Well, with my independence of him. To show him that I'm—what did you call me?—a free agent, and that I don't have to go looking for men to admire me, and when they show they do, I'm going to play along.'

Paula said, only she knew how painfully, 'If he is fond of you, I'd have thought he'd know you are attractive to other men, without needing to be shown.'

'And perhaps he does. But he is so managing with me; if a man looks at me, he practically demands his pedigree and whether his intentions are honourable, and then heads him off as only Gratien can. So when a little devil suggested to me tonight to show him that I could have fun without asking his permission, I staged that act with Guy on purpose. We had been dancing and went out on to the terrace, and when you two came out, I went all flirtatious with Guy, and perhaps he didn't mind making you a bit jealous too——'

'He failed in that,' put in Paula.

'But he probably hoped to. So we played a bit and giggled a lot, and when he showed me his diary, simply crammed with girls' names and telephone numbers, I snatched it and teased him that I wouldn't give it back. And when I ran, he caught me and kissed me as I meant he should, and for Gratien to see.'

'Guy didn't seem very anxious to follow you up,' Paula couldn't resist pointing out.

'No, and he should have done. But it didn't really matter. Tell me, what did Gratien say about us after we had gone?'

'From what he did say, I think you are wrong about him. He didn't seem under any delusions about how attractive you are to men.'

'Oh.' Solange puckered her brows over that. 'But what did he actually say? Did he sound jealous, or angry, or what?'

'As far as I remember he said that he knew you enjoyed your scalp-hunting, and that you picked your victims with flair.'

'Oh,' said Solange again, and then dimpled happily. 'Well, it isn't what I expected,' she admitted. 'But it's nice to know he appreciates that where men are concerned, I can take them or leave them, and that he doesn't have to play policeman to me all the time.'

'In the circumstances, wouldn't you expect him to police you?' asked Paula drily.

'You mean, considering how fond he is of me? But he ought to realise I'm entitled to a lot of fun before I get married or engaged. A girl needs to sample the market, doesn't she? Besides, if you say Gratien didn't seem angry or hurt, there was no harm done tonight, was there? Unless'—Solange paused to study Paula's face—'unless you are only *saying* you aren't jealous or annoyed about its being Guy I choose? But I do assure you it was only by chance; he doesn't care any more for me than I do for him. For everyone in our set knows it is you he is after.'

'To add my name to the others in his diary? Thank you very much,' snapped Paula.

'If it's not there already——! But you wouldn't like that?'

'Do you imagine I would?'

'Shall I tell him so?' Solange's eyes were bright with mischief. 'That you expect to be his one-and-only or not at all? That he must make much more heavy play for you, or you aren't interested?'

'You'll do nothing of the sort!' exclaimed Paula, aghast.

'Oh, I don't know? Dare me——?' Upon which Solange jumped up, swirled her skirts with the air of a bird fluffing its plumage, and chasséed away to join a romp of a dance which was stampeding past.

The next day Gratien's manner with Paula was as collected as if their exchange on the terrace had never happened. And by the cold light of morning even her own dudgeon appeared unreasonable. She had dressed, wanting him to admire her, hadn't she? Yet when he had chosen to express his opinion as he had, she had taken offence and had let him know it. Why? Because with no cause, she had been disappointed, hurt. She should have known, from his cool appraisal of her before he kissed her, that he had had no intention of making his kiss an invitation; an overture to the intimacy her own feelings sought. He had called it a tribute, and that was all it had been, and she had reacted like a child cheated of a treat, and a treat which hadn't even been promised, at that! So it was something of a salve to her pride that he didn't hold it against her, and obviously she had nothing to hold against him. They were back again on the even keel of their everyday contacts and nothing to show of a wishful thinking which she had mistaken for hope.

Gratien had been with the Comte and Comtesse when she went to thank them before leaving. He had left with her; they had collected the others of their party, and on returning to de Tourcy in the small hours they had lingered to compare notes on the evening before going to their rooms.

Milon's verdict was blasé; he had found the bar arrangements only passable, and the girls he had met seemed to be 'the same old lot' whom he had checked over and found wanting last year.

Monique was non-committal about her evening. When Paula asked her if the two Germans with whom they had had supper were new acquaintances, she said they were. The younger one—'Yours,' she described Karl Richter—was rather an earnest bore, but the older one, Hans Brittel, was much more interesting. He said he was glad when Paula had 're-lieved' him and Monique of his friend; he was with a firm of shippers in Bordeaux, and he had suggested coming over to take her out some time, Monique had added, in what Paula felt was a gesture at Gratien not unlike Solange's—intended to show him that if he didn't find her desirable, other men did.

Louise, by contrast, was full of naïve enthusiasm for her evening.

Yes, she had danced, though only in waltzes and

slow foxtrots; not at all in those jigging and head-nodding affairs, in which there seemed no point in having a partner, only to keep him at more than arm's length. No, the highlight for her had been her introduction to a Monsieur Fénelon, staying with his wife at Aragon for a few days.

He was an art connoisseur and dealer who had a gallery in Paris; he had shown an interest in her work and had told her he would like to see some of it.

All diffidence gone temporarily from her manner, Louise claimed, 'He was so pressing that I said I would take some of my best stuff over when I call to thank Julien and Clara on behalf of us all for the party.' She turned to Paula. 'I shall include the sketch I did of you in the kitchen.' And then to Gratien, 'You liked that, didn't you? So careless of me, losing the original rough which I meant Paula should keep. I shall have to do another before she goes away.'

Paula waited, her breath held. Now surely, re-minded, Gratien must recall that he had found the thing and had put it aside, meaning to return it? But she waited in vain for his, 'Oh, I've got that. I found it, and forgot to tell you,' or something simi-lar. But he made no reply at all. Which meant? Well, what could it mean, but that he had helped himself to it deliberately? Why? How she wished they were on equal terms enough to allow her to tell him she knew of its hiding-place, having come upon it by accident. But he was her employer; im-possible to put him in such a false position in front of Louise and the others. The mystery would have to remain one, so far as she was concerned. Since it couldn't have the significance she would like it to have, the explanation must be so trivial that she mustn't allow his silence to matter.

A few days later Louise, naïvely gratified, announced that Monsieur Fénelon had selected some of her drawings to take back to Paris with a view to finding a buyer for them. And on the same day Guy Crespigny apparently decided that he owed Paula an explanation of the scene with Solange.

He went to the château kitchen where Paula was engaged on paperwork, dealing with the accounts for that week's supplies.

'Oh. You're busy,' he stated.

'In fact, yes,' she said, not looking up.

She might have told him she was idly twiddling her thumbs for all the effect her reply had.

'And you are sore too. Piqued with me. And of course I can guess why,' he said, falsely contrite. 'It was that bit of nonsense with Solange the other night, wasn't it? But I assure you, it didn't mean a thing.'

'No, so Solange told me later. And as for its being a nonsense, I couldn't agree more.'

He looked slightly taken aback. 'But before you knew it was only aimed at Gratien, you must have been surprised and a bit hurt that I could——?'

Paula cut in, 'If I ever could have been hurt by you, I'd have been in no more danger of it after Solange told me about the diary you keep of all your alleged 'conquests'' names and telephone numbers, making it likely that mine is there too.'

She intended that as a final *coup de grâce* to his

110

pretensions towards her. But he was so thick-skinned that it signally failed. He moved over to stand behind her chair, lightly massaging her shoulders with his fingertips.

'Ah, so you *were* offended,' he murmured. 'You wouldn't be so upstage with me now if you weren't. I'm not to be forgiven until I've crawled a bit and apologised—that's so, isn't it? The typical woman's trick to bring a man to heel, even when she knows quite well that he is her slave. But so—I crawl, I apologise, I plead guilty'—and he dropped a kiss on the top of her head.

She drew down her shoulders, shrugged off his hands and twisted in her chair to look up at him, frowning. Unless he stepped back she could not push back her chair in order to stand, and it was so, in a closeness which could have been mistaken for intimacy, that Gratien must have seen them when he strode in from the courtyard, an arm round the shoulders of Pierre, the kitchen-boy.

Gratien acknowledged Crespigny with a brief nod, but made no comment on the scene. To Paula he said, 'Quick—hot water in a bowl with disinfectant, and lint and bandages from the first-aid cabinet. Pierre has cut himself at the angle of his thumb with his hand, and I want to staunch the bleeding before I run him into Libourne for an anti-tetanus jab. When you've got the things and while I see to him, will you make him a hot sweet drink—tea, coffee, whatever is handy.'

'Yes, of course. Please——' Paula hinted to Guy, forcing him to stand back for her. He lingered while she busied herself, fetching the things Gratien wanted, then he muttered, 'Seems I've become *de trop* suddenly,' and sauntered out, without having shown any sympathy for the boy.

While Gratien bathed his hand Pierre explained shakily to Paula what had happened.

'Emilie wanted a coop to isolate one of the hens who has gone broody, and she was going to give me five francs to make one. I was chopping some wood to make slats for the floor when the axe slipped and came down on my thumb.' With an attempt at airiness he kissed the fingers of his free hand. '*Au revoir*, good francs. I could have done with you!'

'Lucky for you that you aren't saying *au revoir* to a severed thumb,' Gratien commented, adding to Paula, 'When I came across the yard he was bent double, clutching his hand——'

'And there was blood everywhere,' offered Pierre, not without relish of the drama, for all the pain he must have been in. After thoroughly cleansing his hand Gratien gave it a final douching in ice-cold water and bandaged it deftly, then left Pierre to sip the hot tea Paula had prepared, while he went to fetch the car.

He had been so absorbed in his task that Paula knew she could not have expected him to remark on the scene he had interrupted. She could be confident too that he wouldn't criticise her in front of the boy. But she was irked that his silence had cheated her of the chance to defend herself against what she was sure he must be thinking—despising her for having anything more to do with Crespigny after witnessing his provocative flirtation with Solange. Knowing and tolerating Solange's coquetry as he did, he could forgive her; he wouldn't show any such justice towards herself.

Meanwhile it looked as if Monique had acknowledged defeat of her ambitions where Gratien was concerned. Her new friend, Hans Brittel, had kept his promise to drive over and take her out, and when he had done this on two evenings in the same week and at the weekend, she brightened so much that Paula concluded she had decided to concede victory to Solange, and was glad for her. How she was going to placate her mother's demands that she get Gratien to the point of an engagement before she left le Tourcy could only be a matter of speculation. In any case, in Paula's opinion it had sounded a far-fetched scheme in which she could hardly believe, and she thought Monique was very little troubled about it now, until she surprised the girl in tears over a letter which had come by that morning's post.

When Paula joined her, Monique knuckled her eyes and pretended, too late, that she hadn't been crying. Paula asked gently, 'What is wrong? Can I do anything to help?'

Monique blew her nose and said nothing. Paula pointed to the letter. 'Have you had some bad news in that?'

'Not bad news, no. Upsetting. It's from Maman, and I don't know how to answer it.'

'Why not?'

'Because——' Monique creased and recreased the paper with restless fingers. 'Because she is angry. She says that in my letters now I write always about Hans—"this Brittel", she calls him. She accuses me of letting him spoil my chances with Gratien, and she wants to know why I don't tell her how I am getting on with Gratien. And how can I, when, in the way Maman means, I'm not "getting on" at all? She says that she can't leave Cannes just now, as she is in a delicate situation which has to be handled with care. I don't know what she means by that. But she says she is tempted to come up to see for herself how things stand. And I know what that means,' Monique concluded dully. 'She would somehow manage to freeze Hans out. She has done it before.'

'But you mustn't let your mother freeze him out, and if he matters enough to you, you won't. You are entitled to him as a friend, if nothing more. And if I may say so,' Paula went on, 'I don't think she had the right to send you on such a mission. How could she expect Gratien to ask you to marry him after only six weeks, when he hadn't shown you any particular attention before?'

Monique's sore pride lifted a wilting head. 'He might have done, if I had any of Solange's looks and her silly-doll ways and her clothes,' she said.

'I doubt it,' Paula returned rather brutally. 'Solange has more for Gratien than mere looks. They've got background behind them. They have known each other since Solange was a child; they don't start from scratch with a time limit in which to become—intimate.' Speaking the word hurt, but Paula had braced herself to use it. 'So what are you going to reply to your mother?' she asked Monique.

'I don't know. Perhaps I could pretend I never received her letter?' Monique offered feebly.

'You could try telling her the truth. She will have to learn it sooner or later,' Paula pointed out.

'Oh, I couldn't!'

'As a problem, it won't go away.'

'No, but by not answering Maman I could stall for a while. I can *not* write baldly to her—"I don't want Gratien, and he doesn't want me." She wouldn't understand. Nothing has changed since she sent me here. I *have* to marry well, for her sake. Besides, I don't know yet whether Hans feels the same for me as I do about him. If I did—when ... when I do, it would be easier, with him behind me, to stand up to Maman. Well, wouldn't it?' Monique appealed.

'It might. Is Hans well off?'

'Not particularly, but——'

As Monique broke off indecisively Paula realised that she had failed to convince her that a problem shelved did not necessarily disappear with time gained, so she said no more. Poor Monique! Poor Hans Brittel!—liable to be 'frozen out' by a scheming woman while she tried to marry her daughter to a better financial prospect than he. Paula, wondering how it might all end for Monique, reflected that, with her own time at de Tourcy now whittled down to no more than a week or two, she would probably never learn the outcome. Wherever Monique's battle to fall in love where she chose was ultimately fought, she, Paula, would not be there, taking sides.

Monique's voice, changing the subject, intruded on her thoughts.

'What is this business that Milon and Guy Crespigny are discussing, do you know?' Monique asked.

'Business? Between them? No. Why should I?' said Paula.

'I thought you might—from Guy. They are always together lately, talking it over. I asked Milon what it was, but he only said it was just a scheme they had on, and he wouldn't tell me what it was.'

'Well, Guy is in shipping. The firm he is in exports wines to England. Perhaps he is persuading Milon to apply for a job in the same firm,' Paula suggested.

Monique shrugged. 'Perhaps, and Guy is going over to England for a day or two this week, Milon says. But if it is a question of a job for Milon, I wouldn't back him to keep it for very long. He's not that fond of work. No, somehow I think it is more like something that will make money for them both. But that is only my idea, and I don't really know.'

Nor could Paula imagine what business interests the two could have in common. But their association had nothing to do with her, and she would have thought no more about it if Monique had not brought it up again, surprising Paula that she should be cast in the role of the girl's confidante for the second time in a few days.

Monique worried, 'About Milon and Guy—it's not ordinary business they are hatching. It's——' she bit her lip, seeking the right word—'something underhand.'

'Underhand?' Paula echoed. 'What makes you think so? What do you mean?'

'I don't know.' They were in the garden, gathering flowers for Louise to arrange, and Monique plucked aimlessly at leaves and twigs as she went on, 'I heard them talking together. I don't know what about, except that it couldn't be anything honest, or they wouldn't have said what they did.'

'You heard them, when they didn't know you were listening in?'

'Yes. I was going riding with Milon and I was down at the stables, petting Mirabelle in her stall. I thought Milon hadn't come yet, but in fact he was in the next stall, an empty one, and Guy was with him. And for one thing, they wouldn't have met there, if they hadn't something to hide, would they?' Monique appealed.

'I don't know. Go on,' said Paula.

'Well, Guy said—he sounded annoyed—"If you're going to turn chicken at this stage, we'd better call the whole thing off." And Milon said, "I'm not chicken. But why does it have to be here, not there as well? That way, it wouldn't point just at me." And to that Guy said, "If we run it as I've planned, and if you keep your head, it isn't going to point anywhere in particular. It will just float. As for why not there—I've neither the time nor any reason for organising it at both. Besides, they are not the enemy, and we both know who is." And then he said, "So is it still on or not? Make up your mind, my friend. It's all the same to me".'

'And what did Milon say to that?'

'Nothing. He just grunted and said he supposed I hadn't come. And they both went off together, and I took Mirabelle out alone.'

'Didn't Milon ask you later why you hadn't met him as arranged?'

'I pretended I'd mistaken the time we had fixed; that I had waited for him before going out by myself.'

'So you didn't confront him with what you had heard?'

'No, how could I?' Monique pleaded. 'It might be nothing serious and he'd have laughed in my face. And if it were anything serious——' she broke off, eyes wide, lips quivering. 'Paula, it couldn't be, could it, something near-criminal, like fraud or ... that kind of thing?'

But Paula, puzzled and disturbed as she was, discounted that, to Monique's obvious relief. Paula said, 'No, of course not. I think you are making too much of the little you heard. Listen—Milon wanted to know why "it" had to be laid on "here". That must mean here at de Tourcy, not "there" —at Aragon, surely, from what Guy replied? And "they"—the Comte and Comtesse?—weren't the enemy, but that someone else—Gratien?—was. Which means, I'd say,' she added thoughtfully, 'that they both, Guy and Milon, feel they have some kind of grudge against Gratien and that they're hatching some rather nasty practical joke against him, that's all.'

'Just a mean, silly trick, you think?' queried Monique hopefully. 'And it could be, of course. Milon has been pretty sore with Gratien since he crashed those *douils*——'

'And there's no love lost between Gratien and Guy Crespigny either,' supplied Paula. 'Besides, if Milon sounded as if he didn't want to play, whatever it is may never come off. But if you are still worried, why don't you tell Milon you couldn't help eavesdropping, tell him what you heard and ask him what it meant?'

'If he wouldn't tell me before what the scheme was, he won't now,' Monique objected.

'Then I'd put it out of my mind, if I were you,' Paula advised.

'Yes. All right.' But before they parted Monique had something else to say, and did so diffidently. 'About those threats I made to you about—about Barbizon,' she hesitated, 'I didn't mean them, you know. That is, I don't now. You haven't mentioned it to anyone so far, so I don't think you mean to now.'

'There was no reason why I ever should have done,' Paula pointed out. 'So you needn't have been afraid. It was your secret, and it was all behind you —or so you said.'

'And so it was—is.' Monique shivered with distaste. 'I was a little fool, wasn't I—about Antoine Sallust?'

'Yes,' Paula agreed. 'But only a little fool. Nothing worse.'

The next weekend party was to be the biggest of the season, the number of the guests invited to stay being swelled by those who would be attending the highlight of the occasion, the dinner of the Sunday night.

As, except for a final more intimate affair, it was to be the last of the château's functions before the end of the *vendange*, Paula realised the challenge of it and prepared accordingly. While making her plans she wondered whether Gratien remembered his hint, after her success with that typically English dish, that they must 'do it again some time'. She hadn't tried it again with a main course, but supposing—supposing, she thought mischievously, she should dare to make this dinner an English affair from, as the saying went, 'soup to nuts'?

She began to think along those lines, knowing she would have to present the menu to Gratien as well as to Louise, in order for him to select the appropriate wines to be served.

Now what *was* unmistakably English food? A really light, delicate chicken broth, to prove that English soups need not be dishwatery, with the subtlest trace of herbs to add interest. For the fish —fillet of Dover sole. For the main course, roast crown of pork or lamb, and if a French butcher didn't know how to make the crown, she would do it herself. The pudding—a choice of hot blackberry crumble or Banbury puffs with cream. And the cheese—devotees of Dutch or French cheeses as the guests might be, they should have Stilton—for what could be more English than that?

At the same time she outlined a typically French menu and took both to Louise, to find Louise wrestling with a dilemma of her own.

It had been occasioned by a letter from her patron, Monsieur Fénelon, inviting her, almost in the terms of a royal command, to a three-day exhibition at his Paris gallery where he planned to show some of her pictures for sale. Since it did much for an artist's reputation to be present to meet possible clients, he hoped that Mademoiselle de Tourcy would find it convenient to attend, and if so, Madame Fénelon and he would be happy to welcome her as a guest to their home during the days she was in Paris.

Given the letter to read for herself, Paula said, 'How splendid for you! Of course you will go?'

'Nothing I'd like better. It could be an opening for me,' Louise admitted. 'But look at the dates—Friday, Saturday and Sunday—the weekend.'

'Oh dear,' Paula sympathised. 'You mean the big dinner on the Sunday?'

'And the people who'll be staying. I can't possibly be away. I must be there to act as hostess for Gratien. It's such an important affair for him. No,' Louise took back the letter and refolded it, 'I shall have to make my excuses to Monsieur Fénelon. There's no help for it. Such a pity,' she sighed.

'Have you told your brother about the invitation?' Paula asked.

'Not yet. The letter has only just come. But I have to discuss some other things with him, and I'm going to see him now.' Louise took up the menus and looked them over absently before handing them back. 'You will be consulting him about these?'

'Yes, later. Emilie wants me now,' said Paula.

She had not seen Louise again when she went to Gratien's office in the house and offered him the menus. He had stood when she came in, and remained so while he read both through. He put aside the French one and tapped the other with a finger-nail.

'Your invitation to the marriage we discussed?' he queried, eyebrows lifted.

Her lips twitched to the ghost of a smile, showing she understood. 'If you approve the form of the invitation,' she said demurely.

'Mm. Not just a single course this time—the whole shooting-match.' He read again. 'Well, you've certainly made it convincing. I wonder if a touch of lemon in the soup would be cheating? Anyway, I leave it to you. And Dover sole. And crown roast —yes, showy. And the blackberries—whom are you sending to gather them?'

'I'll go myself, if I have time,' she volunteered. 'You have a wonderful crop here, about which nobody seems to bother.'

'A pity we're preoccupied with the commercial grape at this time of year,' he commented. 'And so —Stilton. Well, it could hardly be anything else, could it?'

'I thought not.'

'And so you are determined to educate us to dine *à l'anglaise*?'

'The marriage with French wines was your suggestion,' she pointed out.

'As you say, and I'll honour it. See me that morning, will you, and I'll tell you my choice.'

She nodded. 'Thank you.' But as she turned to go, he stopped her.

'We have a difficulty regarding the weekend,' he said. 'Has Louise told you about her invitation to Paris?'

'Yes. But she said she couldn't possibly go.'

'And I've said she must go. Which leaves me without a hostess to my guests.'

'Yes. I understand that was why your sister——'

'And so I must find a deputy for her.'

'She has agreed to go, then?'

'I've told you—I've insisted that she must,' he returned a shade impatiently. 'And she agreed willingly enough to my finding a substitute'.

'Oh, I'm glad.' Paula paused, then ventured, 'You will ask Monique to act for her?'

'Not at all. You,' he said.

CHAPTER SEVEN

'Me?' the word jerked from Paula's lips. 'Oh no. You're not serious?'

'Why not? Louise agrees with me. Monique is too young, too gauche, and there is no one else I'd care to ask.'

'One of your older married friends, surely?' Paula murmured.

'I've bidden all the eligible ones as guests. No, you're resident here, and it's entirely reasonable that you should take over for Louise. And don't'— he lifted a hand as she was about to speak—'don't plead that you can't manage the mechanics of being both in the kitchen and in the *salon* and the dining-room, because you've done it before with complete success.'

'That was for just one meal! Louise will be away for three days!'

'No particular problem there. Louise will do all the flowers before she goes, and Monique can bestir herself to help Berthe and the women with the sleeping arrangements. For most of the meals I can play host alone, but you must stand in for Louise on the Sunday night.'

'But I shan't know the people, and they won't know me.'

Gratien smiled slightly. 'I'll furnish you before-hand with a list of names, relationships, habitats and known characteristics. You'll already know the weekenders; you will stand with me to welcome the dinner-guests; Berthe will announce them, and I shall apologise for Louise's absence and introduce you at the same time.'

'As your visiting cook, resident for the *vendange*?'

He looked at her coolly. 'Don't be such an inverted snob,' he advised. 'I shall introduce you by your name, of course. It will be up to you to choose for yourself to tell them whatever you wish about your circumstances here. In any case, they are your chosen role. Why apologise for them?'

'I don't,' she said. 'At Aragon I told anyone who asked me what I did for my living.'

'Well then?'

'Well, there I was just an ordinary guest. Here you are asking me to——'

'To do no more for me than I've every faith you'll carry through successfully—and with charm,' he cut in.

'Thank you.'

He made no comment on her acceptance of the compliment, but as she was about to leave he stopped her again.

'As this will be an affair of my professional contacts and colleagues at a certain level, from Aragon I'm only asking the Comte and Comtesse. But I can include Crespigny too if you like,' he offered.

She wondered how he expected her to take that. 'If you're in doubt, why don't you ask Milon? He is Milon's friend,' she said.

His brows went up. 'Principally Milon's? My mistake. But I forgot—I've had to congratulate you on a deft turn in diplomacy before, haven't I?' he said, spoiling the savour of his compliment and spoiling everything of the prospect before her. He hadn't believed she was disclaiming all interest in Guy Crespigny; he thought she was merely evading his question.

Both Louise and Monique expressed surprise at Gratien's choice of hostess, but whereas Louise was worried that he was laying too much work and responsibility on Paula, Monique was distinctly put out. Though her relations with Paula had improved lately, she obviously felt snubbed and hadn't the poise to conceal it.

'Why you? Why not me?' she wanted to know.

'That's what I asked—why not you. But he thinks you are rather too young,' Paula told her.

'Well, even if he didn't want me, I'd have thought he would ask Solange before you,' Monique said, her tone petulant.

'I don't think he's even asking her to the dinner, which he gives me to understand is mainly a business affair for wine V.I.P.s and their wives.'

'Yes, that's so,' Louise confirmed, 'only Julien and Clara Montdoret are coming from Aragon. There will be very few young people among the guests.'

'Does that mean he won't want Milon or me to be there either?' Monique demanded.

'Oh, that's different. You are staying here——' began Louise. But Monique, piqued and in a nursery 'So there!' mood, cut in, 'Well, he needn't trouble himself, I'm sure. On Sundays there's a midnight movie show at the drive-in cinema just outside Bordeaux, and if we can have the runabout I shall get Milon to take me to it.'

'And I'm sure you can have the runabout,' Louise soothed. 'So do that, why don't you? It will make a nice evening out.'

Meanwhile Paula, with no time to spare for even a day trip to the luxury shops of Bordeaux, had to comb the resources of Libourne for a dress to wear for the evening of the dinner. She hadn't come prepared for social occasions and she felt she literally had nothing suitable for formal affairs but the two gowns in which she had already been seen. This time she knew she must choose something quiet as a foil to the elegance of Gratien's guests—a necessity which fell in very well with Libourne's limitations, since the only dress she could find which she liked and which fitted her was a sober grey silk jersey, long-sleeved and high-necked, almost nunlike in its severity.

Pearls? she debated, trying it on critically back at the château. But only real pearls, which she didn't possess, would do anything for it, she decided. And at least no one could suspect her of trying to outdress Gratien's guests!

Before she left for Paris Louise had wrought magic with her flower arrangements. They were massed in great fan-shapes in the hall and the salon, and the *motif* for the long inlaid walnut dining-table was to be crimson and white chrysanthemums on crimson cross runners, the low bowls of flowers alternating with silver candelabra. To lighten the kitchen and serving work, half a dozen professional waiters had been engaged, leaving Paula with not much more than a supervisor's role on the night itself, before she had to assume the infinitely more demanding one of playing hostess for Gratien.

They had drinks with his resident visitors before going to stand in the hall to greet the dinner guests as they arrived. To each of them Gratien apologised for and explained Louise's absence before introducing Paula to them. A few of them she had already met at Aragon; the Comtesse Montdoret surprised her by kissing her on each cheek. The rest would have been so many names to her, had Gratien not kept his promise of providing her with their potted biographies beforehand. She had memorised the list by heart.

Monsieur and Madame Piche-Seur of the Château Digne. Monsieur a yachting enthusiast in his spare time; Madame the mother of four grown-up sons.

Mademoiselle Spadier, a gold medallist of wine-correspondence and a member of the Bordeaux Academy of wine.

Mynheer Brecht, a Dutch lecturer on wine.

Sir Evan and Lady Wingram; Sir Evan of the fifth generation of English importers. Lady Wingram, Spanish by birth, a gifted concert pianist—and so on. Paula found herself easily and charmingly accepted and she prepared to enjoy her evening—if only all went well with the menu!

So far as she could gather, it did, and without making it the blatant news which she feared, Gratien had allowed the story of her responsibility for it to filter through. He made of it a wry dinner-table joke against himself—he had expected his *haute cuisine* specialist to match her menu to his choice of wine. Yet what did he find? he demanded ruefully of his amused audience—'*She* presents the menu; *I* match the wines!'

They laughed and lifted their glasses to her then, making her blush outwardly with pleasure and glow inwardly with gratitude to him. She tried to let him know it by holding his glance down the length of the table while the others drank their congratulations to her. But the moment passed. She had to look away, and so did he.

Talk flowed interestingly, from one subject to another. For Paula, even the 'shop' she was hearing was coloured by the age-old romance of its subject and of these people's dedication to it—in their own spheres, devotees and craftsmen all.

Then suddenly, within her earshot, an ugly note was struck. She found herself listening to an exchange between two men, a couple of places down the table.

It went, 'Yes. Nasty. What? Oh, the source was English, though how much truth—But one did not expect that to be lifting its evil head again.'

'*Mon dieu*, no.'

'You are talking about——?' A third speaker intervened. 'Yes, I have heard it too. That the stuff is allegedly going into England, and complaints are being lodged.'

'Lodged by whom?'

'By the public to their suppliers, one assumes. As before.'

'And the same trick being played, as then? Provençal second-class goods going out under the Bordeaux label?'

'So one hears. And no suspicions roused until it has been sampled.'

'And names at this end——?'

'——have been named,' the speaker confirmed. He looked about him. 'But ridiculous ones. Honoured ones. Beyond belief as facts.'

'Whose, then?'

A shrug and a shake of the head. 'Oh no, my friend, I am not repeating them. There happens to be a law of slander, and it is by repetition that these foul rumours are spread.'

'Though are they only rumours? One has heard——'

'Nonsense! They must be. The only facts are that spurious consignments are said to have been discovered at the other end—notably in England. For the rest, though they must have come from some consigners at this end, only the wildest speculation has mentioned any names so far, and it seems to me that we should do well to hold our tongues.'

'*En effet*, yes indeed.'

The talk had not spread beyond these few speakers, and from that point they appeared to abandon the subject. But Paula, remembering that something of the same kind of discussion had come up at the first dinner party to which Gratien had bidden her, wondered whether he too had heard these lattest rumours of inferior wines being switched for quality Bordeaux. She thought back to the earlier conversation.

She remembered that Milon hadn't known what

scandals were being discussed, and that Gratien had explained to him how the fraud could be, and had in fact been, worked. By falsified records. By bribed employees of the accused vineyards, if not by culpable owner-bottlers themselves. But she remembered too how Gratien had scorned the suggestion that any reputable château had been or could be involved, and since he must know what he was talking about, it made nonsense of the rather sinister hints she had overheard as to 'honoured' names having been smeared. Absurd of her then to worry lest the name of de Tourcy should be among them ...

A couple of hours later, when the dinner guests had taken their leave, Paula suggested to Gratien that she might gracefully absent herself too. But he said, 'We aren't Royalty who have to leave before anyone else can suggest going to bed. As their host, I must sit these others out, and you must keep me company.'

In fact it was long past midnight when the last of the mellowed weekenders did say their goodnights and went to bed. Paula, fingers at her lips to suppress a yawn, was fully ready to go too, but Gratien offered, 'A cognac while we conduct a post-mortem on the evening?' and tired as she was, she accepted.

The professional waiters had left after they had cleared up, and Gratien had sent the kitchen staff home by taxi, to save them cycling so late at night. The house settled down to an almost tangible silence while he and Paula relaxed, comparing notes on the party's apparent success. In a companionable intimacy she had not achieved with him before, she

131

felt happy and at ease; aware of no disturbing woman-to-man tension while they talked as partners in a common enterprise which had done well.

Later they wondered aloud how Louise had fared in Paris. Gratien mused, 'She has talent which she ought to develop and which deserves notice. But she is top-heavy with loyalty too. Since our mother died, she has effaced whatever ambition she has in favour of being châtelaine here and of being my hostess when I need one. But I'm going to insist that she gets out before it's too late, though goodness knows how often I've argued the matter before now.'

'Perhaps if she comes back with some success in Paris behind her, she'll listen to you now,' Paula suggested.

'Let's hope so. Hitherto she has only argued, "How do I know how good or bad my work is?", and I've had to rest my case on telling her—rather cruelly perhaps—that she isn't unique as a châtelaine, whereas she just might make a unique mark as an artist.'

Paula remembered Louise's own wistful, 'Though I'm so poor at it, Gratien needs me here as his hostess until he marries,' and said, 'Yes, that could hurt her—giving her the idea that she isn't indispensable to you, when she hasn't proved herself in any other way.'

'Well, what other argument has been open to me?' Gratien defended himself. 'Short, that is, of acting instead of wasting words.'

'Acting?'

'By presenting her with the *fait accompli* of my own engagement to marry, with the natural sequence of my wife's becoming mistress here.'

Paula's euphoria faded a little. 'Yes, you could do that,' she agreed. 'And when the time comes, I suppose you will?'

He nodded. 'And though up till now I've always thought in terms of my time, not hers, now you make me wonder whether my time is going to be my own to choose.'

'I make you wonder?'

'When you suggest that she may come back so flushed with success that *she* will be calling the tune of her changing roles, and *I* shall be forced to do the dancing!'

Paula coloured. 'I only suggested she might listen to your argument, not that——'

'—Not that I ought to have ready a bride-in-waiting for her inspection and approval before she decides to leave me flat? Yes, perhaps you are right, and I can afford to wait to play it by ear. To marry in haste, for whatever disinterested purpose, was ever a mistake, wouldn't you say?' As he spoke, his tone flippant, he stood up, his empty glass in his hand. He pointed to hers, but she put her hand over its rim and stood too. He put aside his own as she turned towards the door, and went with her across the hall and up the staircase, his hand as lightly and impersonally on her shoulder as it might have lain upon Louise's.

At the top of the stairs where the corridor led one way to her room and another to his, she paused, only to feel his fingers tighten a little. 'Mayn't I see you home?' he said.

At that the tensions were there again, turning

him from the mere colleague of an evening into a man of whom she was intensely aware. She did not know what his intentions were in seeing her to her room, but when they reached the door, he opened it for her and stood aside. Once across the threshold, she turned back and offered her hand. He took it, then bent to put his lips, lightly and formally, to each of her cheeks—the ordinary Gallic-fashion salute of one comrade to another of either sex.

'Goodnight,' he said, 'and thank you for everything—for all of tonight.'

No intentions then. No assault upon her senses. No deliberate fencing for an advantage which he meant to gain. Nothing. Just the kind of thanks for willing co-operation which he might have expressed equally by a gift of flowers. No more than that. The distance between them hadn't lessened by the width of a thread.

Louise delayed her return for two or three days, and when she did come back it was clear that Paris had done more than tempt her to the hope of a career in professional art. For it appeared that Madame Fénelon, chic and fashion-conscious to a degree, had achieved something which Paula had not dared—she had persuaded Louise to a new image which owed nothing to Louise's outdated ideas on clothes and hair-styles.

The plaited 'earphones' had gone and her hair had been club-cut to stand off squarely from about mid-cheek and to curve in a fringe above the line of her now lightly-pencilled brows. She had travelled out in a hat which had had to spread atop the earphones, and in one of her garish dresses under a drab sand-coloured topcoat. She came home hatless and in a well-cut black trouser suit and cape—a transformation which caused Gratien to tease her, 'You only need an outsize floppy cravat and a velvet beret set askew, and you might have walked straight off the stage of *Bohème*!'

At which she had blushed, claiming that it was all a foolishness into which Madame Fénelon had nagged her. But Paula was convinced that she must know the change lopped ten years from her age, and Paula couldn't believe she wasn't gratified by that.

But more important to Louise was the fact that she had met several of Monsieur Fénelon's clients; he had sold two of her drawings, and some studies she had made of countryside wild life had led to her being approached to illustrate a children's picture-book series.

'These,' she claimed happily, 'I can work on at home here.' But of other suggestions that she would do well to study at a famous college of art—'Naturally, while Gratien needs me here, any such idea I had to turn down,' she added, causing Paula to wish she had the right to tell her how aware Gratien was of the kind of circumstances which would set her free—the inevitability of his engagement to Solange, into which he wasn't to be hustled, but which he had implied was certain, all the same.

Touched by the thought, it was odd, Paula reflected, how each of them had made her their confidante, even though it was only the confidence offered to a stranger—the kind which it was always easiest to give.

Then, a day or two later, the scandal broke the bounds of table and vineyard gossip and found its way into first the local press, and then the national. And though all the reported evidence of fraud by a 'well-known and hitherto respected producer of *petits châteaux* wines' was protected by the guarded word 'alleged', word of mouth had it very quickly that it was the Château de Tourcy which was meant; which was sending inferior stock to England under the château label.

The region was dumbfounded. Other château-owners, equally vulnerable, bombarded Gratien's telephone with advice and questions on how he ought, or meant, to deal with a problem which should it spread could smear them all. Gratien, tight-lipped and unapproachable, scorned most of the advice and answered few of the questions. Convinced as he claimed he was of the innocence of the whole of his work-force, he still subjected every man and woman of them to a relentless grilling; he examined every consignment-sheet for months back; he conducted lightning checks of the crates still waiting in the stores to be shipped; he directed a probe of the backgrounds of any of his workpeople who might have betrayed his trust for money. He worked ceaselessly night and day, and then he went to England.

Every family meal at the château was now an overshadowed affair; the conversation brittle and troubled by the worry which Paula thought must be in all their minds. Gratien spoke little; Louise was apt to begin questions or remarks and leave them to trail away in a sigh; Monique and Milon talked between themselves, but shortly and generally, without touching on the raw subject of the scandal.

Until, on the night before Gratien flew into England, Milon asked him, 'What do you expect to gain by going over?'

'The truth, one hopes,' said Gratien curtly.

'From?'

'The consignees who are supposed to have claimed they have had complaints of the quality of our stuff they have been sent.'

' "Supposed to have claimed"? Don't you know they are claiming it?' Milon queried.

'Only from the rumours at this end. They are going to have to prove to me that spurious wines have been labelled and despatched as ours.'

'And if they say they can prove it?'

'And I know they can't? Then the thing will have to go further. *I* shall take it further—into the courts.'

'Where it had to end up the last time?' Milon prompted.

Gratien looked at him sharply. ' "The last time"? What do you know about that?'

Milon suppressed a yawn. 'Only what you told me yourself; you seemed to think I ought to have heard about it. At dinner one night, soon after we came this year. You were talking about some cases that had gone to law, and the bad name it could give a château even if nothing were proved.'

'Ah yes, I remember now,' said Gratien, making no importance of his agreement.

It was on the day he was due to return when

Monique came to Paula's room. Standing with her back against the door which she had closed behind her, she asked, 'Are you busy?'

'Not just now. Come and sit down,' Paula invited.

Monique came forward but remained standing, her hands hanging emptily at her side, her eyes avoiding Paula's. 'It's something I've thought of,' she said. 'Something rather—awful.'

'Awful? What about?'

'Well, I don't think I really thought it—that is, not consciously. It came to me. Last night I sat bolt upright in bed when I had been asleep, and said aloud, "That's it," and somehow I felt it was, even though I don't know how to believe it of him—of them.'

'Believe what of whom? Do come and sit down and explain,' urged Paula.

Monique sat then, twisting her fingers nervously as she talked. 'Milon and Guy Crespigny,' she said. 'You know I thought they were hatching some scheme between them? To make money, I thought. But now I don't. Now I'm convinced it's something mean, horrible——' She broke off. 'You remember, *you* said you guessed it was some trick they were planning against Gratien, because Milon had a grudge against him, and he had no use for Guy?'

As Paula nodded, 'Yes, well,' Monique went on, 'I let you convince me it was only some kind of joke. But now, whether I dreamed it or really thought it at the moment I woke up, I'm sure it's more. It's —the wine fraud story. They thought it up. They've put it about—for revenge on Gratien!'

Shocked but incredulous, Paula shook her head. 'Oh *no*! How could they? Besides, didn't the rumours come originally from England?'

'The complaints were supposed to, but Guy was over in England before we heard the rumours here,' Monique said meaningly.

'But——'

'And Guy is in public relations for his firm. He gets about, knows newspaper men; he could probably find someone to bribe over there and here.'

'Not here at de Tourcy. Gratien is convinced of that,' Paula maintained.

'I didn't mean he could bribe anyone actually to carry out a fraud shipment. They would have to have inside help for that, and Gratien has proved that nothing like it has been going on. But the *story* —don't you see?' Monique appealed. 'As far as they are concerned, that's been enough to smear Gratien, and they will have been content with that!'

Paula said nothing. She was remembering a minute or two of idle talk with Milon when he had claimed that, unlike self-pitying jealousy, envy was a positive, productive emotion. So had he used his envy of Gratien to serve him in this sordid plot? Gratien was capable, successful; Milon was neither, a drifter. And Gratien had spared him nothing in the matter of the crashed *douils*. Perhaps they had had other clashes too, for all she knew. Reluctant as she was to believe Monique's fears, she supposed it was all possible.

Aloud she said, 'But Guy? He's a friend of the Montdorets. He's staying there. He wouldn't——'

'He is only there on his job,' said Monique. 'He

stays at a different château every vintage. He is just a kind of linkman between his firm of shippers and the vineyard owners. He is no particular friend of the Comte and Comtesse.'

'Oh,' said Paula, who hadn't understood this from Guy or from anyone else. She urged Monique, 'Tell me again just what it was you overheard. Can you remember it all?'

Monique could, and repeated it. At one point Paula stopped her.

'If you're right, Milon wanted Aragon involved too. Why?' she demurred.

'Perhaps he thought the story could do more harm or seem more likely if more than one château was accused.'

'But having put it about successfully, though none of it was true, what could they hope to gain?'

'I suppose it would satisfy them to have blackened Gratien enough.' Monique drew a long deep sigh. 'But if I'm right, and I believe I am, what am I to do about it? What can I do?'

Paula pondered the question. 'Could you bring yourself to tell Gratien what you suspect?' she asked.

Monique shivered as if with cold. 'Of Milon? He's my brother!'

'Gratien has a right to know.'

'Yes, but—could *you* tell him, perhaps?' Monique appealed.

Paula shook her head. 'No. To me it is only hearsay from you. So if you can't go to Gratien, and I can understand you feel you can't, you must tackle Milon yourself. Make him deny it or get the truth from him, and make him go to Gratien as soon as he gets back.'

'I can't force Milon!'

'Then if he's guilty, let him choose between your telling Gratien or his doing so.'

'Threaten him?' Monique shivered again. 'It's an awful thing to accuse him of.'

'If he conspired with Guy Crespigny to do it, it was an awful thing to have done,' Paula commented dryly.

'Yes.' Monique stood. 'Will you come with me when I speak to him?'

'If you want me to,' said Paula. It was the second time the girl had confided in her, and she felt it was the least she could promise. Monique in trouble had an appeal which Monique, bristling with hostility and jealousy, had not. Only a few weeks ago her Barbizon indiscretions had prepared her to regard Paula as her arch-enemy, yet those same weeks in passing had brought them as near to friendship as they were ever likely to come. And if she were right about Milon's mean conspiracy, Paula did not envy either brother or sister the immediate future ahead of them.

CHAPTER EIGHT

RELUCTANT as she was to accuse him, Monique braced herself to tackle Milon before Gratien returned from England, and with Paula as witness, she confronted him early that evening.

As prosecutor she was on the thin ice of only her eavesdropping and her intuition, and at first Milon expressed blank amazement at her story, and then resorted to bluster.

Involving Guy Crespigny without a qualm and admitting their complicity—So what of it? was his reaction. It had only been a joke against Gratien; it had had to have depth and apparent authenticity to get by. Hence Guy's trip to England. The rumours of fraud had to come from there in the first place and, as Monique had guessed, the greasing of some willing palms had laid them on.

They had spread, as had been intended; the scandalised wine-region had spread them further; the operation was successfully on. Perhaps it had gone a bit beyond their control. He, Milon, had expected only the merest whisper of scandal to touch Gratien before Gratien could prove from his records that de Tourcy had nothing to hide. Whereupon the rumours could be expected to die a natural death, as any nine days' wonder did in time; nothing to show for it, no blame to stick, and nobody much the worse for a bit of drama without any substance behind it. In fact, Milon claimed airily, Gratien could probably dine out on the story for months to come.

At that Monique erupted. 'No one the worse for having his reputation blackened and having been put to all the trouble that Gratien has been? No one *the worse*?' she demanded.

'Rubbish,' Milon scorned. 'We only gave him the chance to have a ball, proving his super-efficiency and how nobody could get through his guard.'

'Sick rumours like that would get under anyone's guard,' Monique claimed with spirit. 'But why, Milon—why? And whose idea was it? Yours or Guy Crespigny's?'

'Mine, in the first place, I suppose.'

'And you suggested it to him?'

'We kicked it around between us, and it seemed to have some possibilities and appeal. But only as a joke, nothing more.'

'A joke you would have admitted to in the end— or not?'

Milon shrugged. 'Not—what do you think? I've told you, we expected it to die a natural death, and it wouldn't have done either Guy or me any good to be there at the bierside as chief mourners, would it?'

'I'll say it wouldn't!' began Monique vehemently. 'You——' She broke off and turned to look over her shoulder. Unheard by any of them, Gratien had come into the room. He glanced at each of them in turn, then back at Milon. He threw his brief-case into a chair and addressed the boy. 'And so—how much were you implicated in all this—if you were?' he asked.

143

At that point, feeling that this was a family affair and that Monique, roused, had not needed her moral support, Paula made a move to go. But Gratien stopped her.

'I could want to ask you the same question presently,' he said. 'Monique too. So please stay, both of you.'

They glanced at each other and stayed. Gratien said to Milon, 'Well, I've heard the whole story of Crespigny's hand in this pretty despicable plot. Not from him, but in England. So now, considering your association with him, do I conclude you were in it too?'

Milon nodded sullenly.

'I see. And your part in it was———?'

'The same as his, you could say. But it only started as a joke. You claimed to be so sure that nothing of the sort could ever touch you, and we thought that a few doubts on that for a week or two wouldn't do you any harm.'

'I see. You grudged my knowing that I wasn't fool enough to risk corruption, and that I was pretty well as certain I had the loyalty of everyone on the estate too? Well, congratulations if you got the results you hoped for, though you can't expect me to sympathise if you were disappointed. Meanwhile, perhaps I may wonder why you considered I deserved even the little "harm" that the story has done me while it has gone the rounds?'

But to that Milon said nothing, and Gratien did not press the question. Instead he asked, 'What were you and Monique arguing about when I came in?'

'About the story. She seems to have found out we were responsible, and——'

'Then you weren't in it as well?' Gratien demanded of Monique.

'Of course not!'

'Nor you?' His glance and his question flashed at Paula, who started and coloured as she met his accusing eyes.

'*I*?' She felt her very emphasis should give him enough answer, but it seemed he wasn't satisfied. 'In no one's confidence, then?' he pressed. 'Not in Milon's? Nor in Crespigny's? No cosy sharing of the alleged "joke" at all?'

Still staring at him, she opened her lips to deny, 'None', but Monique's protests of her own innocence outvoiced her, and she was left to question whether he believed her or not as he turned back to Milon with an unhelpful, 'Well?'

'Well, what?' Milon blustered.

'What next? Personally I'd appreciate a few telling words with your friend Crespigny, so perhaps you will go and telephone him to tell him so. After that——'

'You want him to come over here? Supposing he refuses?'

Gratien said coolly, 'I leave it to you as to how you impress on him that he shouldn't refuse; that I'm not taking his refusal as an answer.'

Milon hesitated. 'And I suppose you'll want me —both of us'—he glanced at Monique—'to leave de Tourcy?'

'That's for you to choose,' Gratien told him. 'If

you are going to be embarrassed by staying, you'll go. If not, I'm not driving either of you out. But now—Crespigny, if you please. Get him.'

When Milon had left the room Monique appealed, 'Did you mean that, Gratien? That you won't insist on our going home before we were due to, however angry you must be with Milon?'

'You heard me tell him—he can go or not, as he sees fit. Anyway, there's no suggestion that you should have to choose; I hope you'll stay for as long as we invited you. You will?'

'Oh, *please*!'

Gratien smiled. 'You don't want to go before-times?'

'Well, not in any kind of disgrace. Maman wouldn't understand. She would be so angry.'

'There'd be no disgrace where you are concerned. Milon can admit as much as he cares to, or nothing. Your mother won't hear a word on the subject from me,' Gratien promised.

'She will know about it. It has been in the papers,' Monique said miserably.

'But not about Milon's involvement in it. That need go no further than this house and Aragon. I can trust the Montdorets to hold their tongues. Meanwhile,' Gratien smiled again, 'may I say I doubt whether the risk of your mother's anger is either the only or the real reason for your not wanting to go home just yet?'

Monique blushed and looked away.

'Some unfinished business with one Hans Brittel was what I meant,' he went on. 'H'm?'

'Well——'

He went over to her and put an arm about her shoulders in a brotherly gesture which, when she was pledged to 'catch' him, she would have either resented or misunderstood, Paula reflected. Now she only looked up at him gratefully.

'Stay just as long as the business is likely to take,' he said. 'You're welcome.'

He picked up his brief-case, preparatory to accompanying them both from the room. But Paula lingered.

'May I speak to you, please?' she asked him.

He turned, allowing Monique to go on. 'Yes?'

'It's just,' she said, 'that I'm not sure whether you believed my denial of having heard anything about all this from Guy Crespigny, so I'd like to repeat it, if I may.'

'You needn't. I heard you. I took it you were giving me your word, and I accept that.'

'Thank you. I'm glad. Because I was going to say that if you had any doubts about it, you would be fully within your rights in dismissing me, and I'd go.'

He nodded slowly. 'Of course you would go—if I had any reason for dismissing you. Which, over this affair, I obviously haven't.'

It wasn't enough. She hadn't held him back just for this brittle exchange which gave her no opening for telling him what she really wanted him to know. She said a little desperately, 'It's only obvious to me, if I can believe I've convinced you there was never any question of my being in Guy Crespigny's confidence. About this, or about anything else. We're not, and never have been, on any kind of intimate terms. I don't find him attractive. I'm not flattered by his attentions. I've just about tolerated them, and that's all. So if you've ever supposed otherwise, you've been wrong.'

'You must know I've supposed otherwise. And I don't remember your having been at any pains to set the record straight before now.'

'I had no reason to think you would be interested.'

'No? I thought I'd made it clear from the beginning that I didn't find him a very desirable character?'

'That could have been just personal prejudice.'

'Prejudice or not, you'll agree now that I had good reason for it?'

She nodded. 'That I agree was what I wanted you to know.'

It was. But wanting more than that, she had listened in vain for him to tell her warmly that he was glad she was proof against Crespigny's gallantries. She would have liked him to say—she wasn't sure what, except that it should be something which would show his interest in what she had told him was personal, even curious——

And then suddenly he was saying it. 'And if you've always been as indifferent to the man as you claim, I'm wondering why you allowed Solange to tell him you were disappointed with the lack of fire in his courtship of you?'

Paula stared, aghast. 'Solange told him that?'

'In my hearing.'

'But——!' Suddenly Paula had remembered Solange's mischievous 'Dare me——?' which she had

148

not taken up, and which she had never supposed the girl had meant seriously. She went on, 'Solange had no right to say anything of the sort. It wasn't true, and she at least has known, ever since the night of the ball at Aragon, that Crespigny has never been of the slightest interest to me.'

'Ah, that night——' Gratien said cryptically.

'Yes, that night. She did threaten in joke that she meant to tease him about me, but I couldn't believe she would.'

Gratien said, 'You don't know Solange. Mischievous intrigue—usually pretty harmless—is meat and drink to her. So you're telling me she used her over-fertile imagination to fake this story to stimulate Crespigny to do better in your eyes?'

Paula said flatly, 'I'm telling you, whether or not you believe me.'

He looked at her then with the deep, considering scrutiny he had sometimes used on her before. 'I believe you,' he said. 'Somehow a message like that from you to any man isn't in character. As for Solange, she deserves a sound spanking, and if I weren't only *in loco parentis* to her while she is here, I might well be tempted to administer it.'

Puzzled, Paula echoed, '*In loco parentis?* You are not her guardian!'

He shook his head, agreeing. 'No. Wrongly quoted description. The Montdorets are that to her. I'm just——' He didn't finish the phrase and didn't add anything to it.

But—guardian! A stand-in for her parents! However promptly he had disclaimed the phrase, it had been his first thought in describing his relationship to Solange. So might it not be the true one, after all? Was it perhaps that, in marrying a beloved child wife, he saw himself in the role of father figure and indulgent protector as well as husband? *Was* it? If only he had finished the sentence, the certainty of what he was to Solange might be easier to bear than the doubt, Paula thought.

After an interview on which Gratien did not comment in Paula's hearing, Guy Crespigny left the Château Aragon, not to return. Milon also decided to leave de Tourcy. Monique, reassured that she was still welcome, did not go with him.

'I don't know what he will tell Maman as to why he has gone home early,' she worried to Paula. 'The one thing I'm sure he will be afraid to tell her will be the truth.' But in fact, from a laconic postcard he sent her a day or two later, it appeared he had shelved the problem. He had joined a school friend's family for an autumn camping trip to Italy instead of returning yet to the Riviera. Monique would probably be home herself before he showed up there ...

The *vendange* was almost over now and ahead for Paula lay the last private party the château would give. When the last vines had been stripped and the last juices processed, there would be a final party both for and given by the vineyard workers. It was held in the great main wine store, the *chai*, financed by the château, arranged and catered for by the vintagers themselves.

'For that one night,' Louise told Paula, 'we are

the guests and they are the hosts. You should enjoy sitting down to a meal for which you haven't the responsibility, and as for me, I am always relieved when, for another ten months, we can entertain only our own friends, and even them, just a few at a time. Meanwhile, here is the list of people coming for this weekend and to dinner; not a very formidable lot this time; most of them neighbours and people we especially like.'

Paula scanned the list of names, the Montdorets and Solange and Hans Brittel among them. She stopped at another completely unexpected but familiar one. She looked up.

'Monsieur Napoule le Tyr? Is he a friend of yours, then?' she asked.

'Of Gratien's, yes indeed. We have known him for a long time; at first in a business way. He has a great deal of influence with Paris restaurateurs and writers on wine subjects, but lately we have saved him up for our more intimate parties, and he always comes,' said Louise.

'I know him too. I graduated from his School of Gastronomy, you know,' Paula mentioned.

Louise nodded. 'So your diploma said, I remember. I think it impressed Gratien. But hasn't he ever told you we know Napoule?'

'I don't think so,' said Paula. 'Of course, to us students Monsieur le Tyr was the Very Great Man; we quaked in our shoes if he looked our way, and if he addressed us——! But when I got my diploma, he promised me an excellent reference if he were approached for one, and I should like to meet him again. Would it be asking too much,' she added, 'if you would mention my name to him while he is here?'

'But of course you will meet him,' said Louise. 'He will be here for the weekend, and you will be one of us as usual. And I know Gratien will expect you to dine on the night our neighbours join us. You have done it before, so you will be able to arrange it, won't you?'

Pleased, Paula said she could, with Emilie's willing help, and Louise went on to ask whether she planned to go straight on to another job when she left the château at the end of the *vendange*.

Reasonable as the question was, it almost startled Paula, who had made no plans for her immediate future. She should have done. In the closing stages of any other job, except in the case of her precipitate departure from Barbizon, she had always envisaged what she meant to do next. But these weeks which had meant to much to her professionally and emotionally appeared like an island in time, cut off from the past and equally cut off from a future into which she would have to plunge eventually. Doing what? Going where? She did not know.

She told Louise laughingly, 'In fact, I've been so happy here and you have made me so much at home that I've done nothing yet about another post. I shall go back to Paris and see what turns up. I shall be too late to join a school for the autumn term; I may advertise for some freelance catering for luncheons and dinners, as I did in England.'

'And if you did, and continued with it, might that leave you free to come to us again next year?'

asked Louise eagerly. 'For I assure you, you have been the greatest success as well as'—she paused and coloured—'a very great friend to me. Gratien too admires you tremendously. He thinks you are a woman in a thousand, I know. So if perhaps next year——?'

Next year—when Solange would probably be the châtelaine of de Tourcy, and Louise herself, freed of her obligations to it and to Gratien, might be happily engaged on a career of her own? No, there could be no next year's *vendange* for Paula at the Château de Tourcy, nor anywhere in the Bordeaux region. The island must remain an island and a bittersweet memory, no more. She managed to evade Louise's hopeful question with a 'Yes, perhaps,' which appeared to satisfy Louise, however falsely it rang in her own ears.

As it happened, when the other weekend guests arrived Napoule le Tyr was not among them. He had telephoned, Louise told Paula, that he had been delayed, but that he hoped to travel from Paris to the château in time for dinner on Saturday, the night of the party for the de Tourcys' neighbour-hood friends. So that, busy until the last minute with the dinner arrangements, Paula did not see him until she joined Gratien's guests in the *salon*, gathered there for aperitifs before the meal.

She did not hope he would recognise her, so she must wait until Louise found time and opportunity to introduce her. But Louise, newly self-possessed after her Paris début, was talking and laughing with her other guests, and a few minutes after Paula's arrival the party went in to dinner. Louise had remembered her promise, however. Before they sat down she isolated Napoule le Tyr and brought him to meet Paula, and when they took their places at table Paula found him exactly opposite to her.

They each had their own partners to talk to, but he had claimed to remember her well as one of his most able students, and when the meal was under way and there was one of those inexplicable silences common to all general conversation, he looked across at her and said,

'I'm glad to find you believe in varying your experience, Mademoiselle Raymond. It was certainly a delightful surprise to meet you here, doing *haute cuisine*. For the last I heard of you, you were teaching dietetics to schools. Isn't that so?'

Paula said, 'Yes. I had two years at a finishing-school at Vincennes. But how did you know?'

'Ah, I didn't know about Vincennes. Your employers there didn't refer back to me. It was your next employer who did. You had furnished her with your diploma, but she wanted a reference from me too. Now let me see'—he tapped the end of his long nose in thought—'yes, a Madame Sallust. In Barbizon. You joined her school staff at Easter, I believe? Her finishing-school for young ladies?'

For Paula it was as if, momentarily, time had stopped and though one or two people had begun to talk again among themselves, as if she had to speak her agreement into a silence which went on and on, and which made each reluctant word audible to the whole table. She said, 'Yes, I was at Madame Sallust's school for the summer term,' and was at once aware of the electric current of dismay and fear which flowed to her from Monique, seated a few places down the table.

Their eyes met. In Monique's there was entreaty, a look of panic which begged, 'Don't say any more. Gloss it over. Talk about something else!' But already an exchange which would have have had no significance to most people there had been noted by both Gratien and Louise, as their questioning glances showed.

Louise spoke first. 'You were at Barbizon before you came to us? But, Monique dear, wasn't Madame Sallust's where you were too?' And as Monique nodded with a throaty 'Yes', Gratien addressed Paula casually, far too casually for her comfort. 'Do you know, I hadn't realised that you and Monique would have met before you both joined us here?' he said, making nothing of a revelation which at least must have surprised him and which, had he but known it, threatened to tear Monique's world apart.

For her part, Paula breathed again. There would be questions later—there must be. But for the moment she knew both he and Louise were too well bred to embarrass their guests by conducting an inquiry as to the hows and whys of Barbizon. The party would go on its smooth sociable way and no one would guess at the sinister undercurrents running for two of its number. Paula sent a reassuring glance at Monique before she resumed talking with her own neighbour. But her thoughts ran ahead of the evening; ahead of this reprieve she and Monique had gained. For she had no doubt of the ordeal before them. Gratien's smooth dismissal of the subject had shown a false lack of interest.

He would ask the questions and would want them answered—as to why neither she nor Monique had evinced any gleam of recognition on their meeting. For all he knew, the solution might be quite innocent. But he would still want to know why.

She did not expect he would bring up the subject again that night, but to avoid the chance of it she hoped she could make her after-dinner duties in the kitchen her excuse for leaving the party soon after it had adjourned to the *salon* for coffee. But in this she was foiled for a time by being waylaid by the Comtesse.

'As soon as the *vendange* is over, Julien and I are taking a holiday in Biarritz. And you, my dear, will be leaving too?' the Comtesse asked.

'Yes. At about the same time,' said Paula.

The Comtesse sighed. 'It is a too busy, anxious season, but I am always a little sad when it is over. One misses the young people who gather for it— the young journalists, the junior executives, one's own young guests. For me, for instance—Solange, a dear child to have about the house, so bright, so mischievous, and collecting and discarding so many young men! Since her schooldays—and she comes to us almost every year—her path has been littered with broken romances of very short duration, leaving her quite unscathed and heartwhole still. So much so that when she does engage herself seriously, I shall hardly believe it until I see her at the altar. One hopes this for her, of course, and one can't help making wishful plans for her. In fact, nothing would more delight Julien and me than that she should have met and known her future husband through us. But there!—she is like a piece of quick-silver, not to be caught until she wills it, however honourable and indulgent and loving the man.'

And than that, without mentioning his name, you could hardly tell me more clearly that you hope the man may be Gratien, thought Paula. Aloud she said lightly, 'Well, this year at least, her pins in St Emilion's fountain forecast that she would be married.'

They both laughed, and when someone else came to join them Paula excused herself. 'But it is only *au revoir*, one hopes?' said the Comtesse. 'We shall see you again next year?'

'I hope too that it is only *au revoir*,' Paula replied, making that her answer to both questions.

As they left the dining-room Monique had pressed forward to catch at her hand; held it low out of sight. Monique had said urgently. 'I must see you. May I come to your room afterwards?' And Paula had not been long there when Monique arrived.

Frightened and on the defensive, 'Why didn't you tell that man le Tyr that he had made a mistake? That Madame Sallust must have written to him about someone else, or that he had mistaken her name and the place—anything?'

Paula said, 'Don't be silly. He had remembered me on sight, and he had it all so pat that I couldn't have claimed he hadn't got the rest correctly. And if I had argued, it wouldn't have passed off as it did.'

'But it didn't pass off for Gratien! You could almost see him filing it "for future reference". And try telling him that our reason for keeping it secret is none of his business—just try it, that's all! So what are we going to say?'

'The truth, I suppose.'

'What truth?' snapped Monique.

'There is only one—that you didn't want it known that we had been at Barbizon together, and so I agreed to say nothing.'

'He won't leave it there! He will want to know what I was hiding, and I dare you to tell him. If you do, I'll—I'll——' the girl declared wildly.

Paula said quietly. 'Look, don't get hysterical. For hasn't the situation altered? You didn't want him to know about your affair with Antoine Sallust because your mother had insisted you had to try to marry him. But with little chance of that, as I think you know, what would it matter if I told him you had been a bit indiscreet at Barbizon—no details —and didn't want your mother to know?'

'Matter? Of course it would matter. I daren't risk his knowing anything of which he or Louise could give a hint to Maman.'

'Why should either of them do that?' queried Paula.

'They might not realise they had, but Maman is so shrewd that she would suspect they had learned something against me, which was why I hadn't been able to work up any romance with Gratien. Besides, there is Hans. He heard the bit between you and Monsieur le Tyr, and Gratien and Louise. He is bound to ask me what it meant, and I couldn't bear to tell him about——' Monique paused and met Paula's glance with calculation in her eyes.

'No,' she said slowly, 'no. I'm not going to be the one to take the blame for keeping it secret. You must.'

'I?' exclaimed Paula. 'I had no cause!'

'And who is to know that, if I say it was you who asked me to say nothing, not I you?'

'But you won't. You couldn't. It wouldn't be the truth.'

'All the same, you didn't want Gratien to know about Barbizon, or you would have told him you were there before I arrived. Don't you remember how surprised I was that you hadn't? So you had something to hide, and you asked me to co-operate. That's what I shall say.'

'I had nothing to hide!'

'Not even that you were accused, however wrongly, of playing around with Antoine Sallust and of stealing Madame's brooch, and that though you weren't dismissed, you left in a hurry? Don't you think Gratien and Louise had a right to hear about that before they gave you this job?' Monique pressed.

'As I was completely innocent and did leave of my own accord, I didn't consider I need say anything about it.'

'But when Gratien starts asking questions, what are you going to tell him? The truth—by accusing me? If you do, I shall tell *my* story, and that will make it my word against yours, as I warned you before.'

'Don't worry,' said Paula wearily. 'When he questions me, I shall do what you say is impossible—I shall have to admit that our not acknowledging each other was deliberate, but I shall say that our reason was private, and leave it at that.'

'Whetting his curiosity all the more!'

'Perhaps. But if you say the same, he must accept it. They can't force the details from us.'

'You really think you can get away with it?' asked Monique, sounding a shade less truculent.

'I shall have to try, shan't I?' said Paula. 'If the truth can't be told, it's the only way. And if Gratien accepts that we have a right to tell them nothing, I think Louise will accept it too.'

Privately she had little more hope than had Monique that she could forestall Gratien's probing, but when it came his approach was casual.

'An odd coincidence—Napoule le Tyr's having given you a reference to that school at Barbizon where Monique was in her last year?' he remarked.

'Yes, wasn't it?' said Paula, though distrusting his nonchalance.

'Even more odd, surely, that neither of you seemed to recognise the other when you met again here?'

There was nothing casual about that. To Paula it signalled danger. She said carefully, 'We did recognise each other, in fact.'

'As I know you must have done. But you gave no sign of it. You have never mentioned it since.'

'No. We—agreed that we needn't.'

'You were in touch, then, before you both arrived here?'

'No. In Bordeaux it was a surprise meeting for us both.'

'Then it must have been at sight that you man-

160

aged a silent promise to each other and confirmed it later?'

'Something like that. But we had our private reasons.'

He seemed to be waiting for her to go on to enlarge upon that, but when she did not he asked,

'And even now you don't feel under any obligation to clear up the mystery, if only for the sake of courtesy to Louise and me?'

'Not really, no.' That sounded too offhand, and she regretted it when he said in a harder tone, 'Your private reasons prevented your mentioning, when we engaged you, that you had had a later job than the one at Vincennes?'

'You didn't ask me specifically. You asked whether my testimonial from the Mesdames Varron was the latest one I had, and it was.'

'If I remember, you let me assume that that was also your latest job.'

'When you did, it didn't seem important to correct you. You appeared satisfied with the credentials I had.'

'So keeping the fact from us only became important with the strange chance of your meeting Monique again?'

There was no way out. 'Yes,' Paula said.

'Because you both knew there was something to hide about Barbizon?'

She moistened her dry lips. 'Because,' she said, 'whatever there was, it had been resolved since and wasn't the concern of anyone else, we felt.'

'I see. Then if you are still set upon this out-of-date mystery, I'm to take it that there is nothing more to be said?'

'Please. And Monique feels the same—that it is solely our affair, and always was.'

'In other words, you've agreed to give the same answers to the same impertinent questions? Very well, I'll waste no time asking them of her and I'll advise Louise to ask none either.'

The cutting note in his voice told Paula that he was letting her win at the price of his trust and the sense of friendly partnership which was all of him she had ever had to treasure. But before he left her he turned back at the door of the room.

'Tell me,' he asked, as if with a change of subject, 'at that school in Barbizon, did you have an assistant or a superior in the same line as yourself?'

She stared at him. 'Teaching dietetics? No, I was the only person who did.'

'So?' That was all. She watched his brows draw together in a frown of reluctant belief, but without another word he went on his way, leaving her to realise the drift of his cryptic question and to remember; to know with cold certainty that he had remembered too——

Monique at that first dinner they had shared at de Tourcy, saying, '*We had a woman who lectured us about cooking. But she left in some kind of disgrace before the end of the term.*' Monique; emboldened by the promise of silence which she had wrung from Paula, affording herself spite, in the belief that her secret was safe!

And with one adroit, apparently irrelevant question, Gratien had satisfied himself—wrongly—that

162

he knew the truth of their secrecy; perhaps, from the way he had frowned, didn't want to believe that the disgrace had been Paula's, but did believe it all the same. He had left her defenceless against an accusation which had not even been spoken, and the only way out for her was by telling the real truth—which she must not.

CHAPTER NINE

THOUGH Gratien must have reported something of
that interview to Louise, he had evidently advised
her against asking her own questions of either
Paula or Monique, and for this Paula was grate-
ful. The ensuing icy climate between him and herself was hardly to be borne, but during the last few
days of her stay at the château she could manage to
see less of him than of Louise, who remained as
gentle and approachable as ever.

Almost hourly she expected Gratien to invite her
to volunteer an answer to his final enigmatic comment, for she was convinced he was aware that she
had taken its meaning. But he said nothing, and
nor could she, for very shame at admitting to him
that she had been suspected of petty theft and worse,
with the alternative of betraying Monique to him
—equally unthinkable. He must believe what he
would. When they parted next week, none of it
must matter any more.

She was able to satisfy Monique that all was as
well as they could hope. She told the girl that though
Gratien had obviously expected the common
courtesy of their explaining themselves, he had reluctantly accepted their right to their reserves on
the subject of Barbizon. He had said that neither
he nor Louise would pursue it any further, leaving
Monique incredulous but relieved. Paula did not

report to her how the interview had ended, and found Monique's embarrassed thanks rewarding. Monique would never know all that her panic-driven insistence on silence had cost Paula. But as far as she was able, Monique did her best to make amends.

She was increasingly happy herself. She was seeing Hans Brittel often, and either he had not questioned her or she had managed to satisfy him with some explanation of the pact between herself and Paula. For they had the air of everything being sunny upon their horizon, and for the time being Monique seemed even to have lost her fear of her mother's reaction to her affair with Hans. Physically she had blossomed too; her eyes laughed more and her sullen mouth lost its droop. Now she did not merit the description *jolie-laide*—she was positively and youthfully *jolie*.

Paula's last days hastened on too fast. Once, shopping in Libourne, she met Solange, who invited her to coffee on the Square. Solange said she would be leaving Aragon on the day after the château's own vintagers' party, and a day or two before the Comte and Comtesse left for Biarritz.

'Then in December I am going with Maman to the Canary Isles for Christmas and most of January,' Solange added. 'I am trying to persuade Gratien to come too. But he is tiresome and won't give me a Yes or No. He has to "wait on events", he says. And when I ask, what events—business or personal, he says, "Perhaps both; perhaps neither", and anyway he has to arrange to free Louise to go to Paris for painting.'

This airy confidence puzzled Paula, remembering the night of her rare closeness to Gratien, when he had joked about his need to marry before Louise's loyalty would allow her to leave him for the sake of her own career. He had debated then that he might have to present Louise with the fact of his engagement or his marriage in order to persuade her to go. And if this were so, what was he waiting for, allowing Solange to escape him, when surely he himself had the ordering of the 'events' which would solve the problem for him? He couldn't doubt that he meant to ask Solange to marry him, or that she might accept him—could he?

For something to say, Paula asked if Gratien visited often at Solange's home.

'Oh yes,' said Solange. 'My people like him and he likes them. They say I tease him and try his patience too much, and perhaps I do. But it's rather fun, isn't it, to see how far you can provoke a man until he turns and rends you?'

'I don't know that I've ever tried it,' said Paula drily.

'Risked it, you mean,' Solange quipped back. 'And it *is* a risk with a man like Gratien. When he is really angry, I can imagine he could carve one into little pieces and toss them over his shoulder. But I'm in rather a special position and I've never had to worry. Ever since'—the rosebud mouth simpered at the memory—'he pulled my hair quite savagely, and I bit him in return.'

'How long ago was that?' Paula asked.

'Oh, about the first time I came here. I had bitten him on the ball of his thumb, and all he did was to offer me the other thumb, and he bore no malice at all. And it has been the same ever since. Even when I am quite horrid, he indulges me and tolerates me. Tells himself he understands me, I think, and being understood, whichever way one jumps, can be a bit of a bore. To the point, in fact, where I long to do something so outrageous that he would have to be angry, and I could watch the result.' Solange then looked at her watch, stood, and said she must go, leaving Paula, as she went to find her own parked car, thinking that she had experience enough to describe the 'result'.

No ostentatious 'carving up' or searing firebrands of displeasure. Even no overt accusations. Just a cold question of which the questioner assumed he knew the answer, and after that a looking through and looking around the accused one, and the polite indifference of a judge who didn't care whether or not he heard both sides of a case. That was Gratien angry, she could have told Solange, and that if she cared anything for him, it would hurt.

Meanwhile Paula had had to face the fact of her own imminent departure. She had advised the concierge of her Paris studio apartment as to the day of her return and had put an advertisement in a Paris journal, offering her services as a visiting caterer for winter-season social occasions. Immediately after that chilly interview with Gratien she had been tempted to leave at once, since by going she would inconvenience no one and abandon no duties undone. But pride steeled her against the impulse to run away. She had been engaged for the length of the *vendage* which the vintagers' party would end, and she would see her contract out.

Three more days to the party ... then two ... then the one which was to stage a surprise which she was glad not to have missed. It began when, as once before, she came upon Monique reading a letter from her mother, but this time Monique was giggling hysterically over it.

'From Maman,' she chortled, waving the paper at Paula. 'You'll never believe—Or perhaps, of her one can. She has been so long in search of security and leisure and when it escaped her, she turned quite hard. But now she has engaged herself to marry an Algerian oil magnate, she claims she loves him and wouldn't care if he hadn't a sou, though he is rolling in wealth, of course.' Monique paused to address the letter as if it were her mother in person. 'Maman, Maman, *chérie*,' she said to it, 'how I should like to believe you, and how I know I can't!'

'Perhaps you can,' suggested Paula.

Monique shook her head. 'Not easy. I know Maman. She enjoys creating an image of herself, but she changes it as often as she would like to be able to discard any outfit she has had to wear more than twice.'

'Well, if the man is to be your stepfather, perhaps you had better try to believe that she will make this image last,' said Paula.

'Oh, I'll try,' Monique conceded. 'And of course I would like to believe her. Poor Maman, she has worked so hard to keep her head above water, and I'm not the one to spike her guns now she is on the crest of the wave.' She giggled lightheartedly.

'That's a metaphor, isn't it—a good one?'

'Slightly mixed, but let it pass,' smiled Paula.

'And she—Maman—doesn't try to pretend about what her marrying money will mean to Milon and me. She comes straight out with it. Listen——' Monique read aloud——

' "And so Milon, the ingrate who hasn't bothered to come near me since he became bored with de Tourcy and left, can now waste several more years at university if he pleases. And you, *chérie*, who couldn't try to charm Gratien in order to save me worry for your future, need not trouble yourself any more. If your new beau does not prove the devoted suitor you think he is, I am sure I can persuade my Fabian to settle something on you— you will not want for money, I assure you. Or if this affair between you and this Brittel does have some meaning for you, bring him to see me when you come home, and Fabian and I will look him over——" '

Monique looked up at Paula. 'You see how she deludes herself that it was *my* future she was concerned over, with Gratien? Whereas, when she sent me here, she spelled it out that it was she who could be saved from poverty and the shame of debt if I could only catch Gratien. Now she is being gracious about accepting Hans.' Folding the letter, Monique said again, 'Poor Maman. She believes what she wants to believe at any given time. It is a gift.'

Paula said, 'Well, at least Hans now has her blessing.'

'Not that it would matter now if he hadn't. I—I think he is serious about me.'

'And you about him?' Paula asked unnecessarily.

'Unbelievably,' said Monique with fervour.

Louise and Paula dined alone that night. Monique was out, supposedly with Hans, and Louise thought Gratien meant to dine at Aragon, though he hadn't said so. For Paula it had been a day of 'last times'. In the afternoon she had driven over to St Emilion to say goodbye to it; she had returned as dusk was falling and had walked round the gardens and through the deserted vineyards where the vine leaves were already beginning to yellow and to wrinkle, their season's work done and with their falling, releasing the vines to their long winter sleep. By contrast in the *chai* there was a hum of activity—not now of work, but of the festive arrangements for tomorrow's party. Before dinner she had collected her cookery books from the kitchen; she would stage-manage no more meals for the de Tourcy tables. The day after tomorrow she was going to part from Emilie and Rosalie and Pierre as from friends.

At dinner Louise was wistful about her leaving. 'It is going to be quite strange without you. You have become so much one of us,' she said.

'Only because you have made me so,' Paula told her.

'But you could have made it difficult. I suppose——' Louise hesitated, 'you must go now? You wouldn't consider staying with us for a few days' real holiday?'

But Paula, though lacking an ironclad reason for her departure, pretended she had one—not entirely convincing Louise, she realised, when the latter questioned,

'It's not—forgive me—that you have had a difference with Gratien, and feel you don't care to stay, or wouldn't be welcome?'

A 'difference' with Gratien—the understatement of the year! thought Paula. 'Not exactly a difference,' she told Louise. 'Why?'

'Well, because of his manner with you, ever since that little mystery you and Monique made of your having met before at Barbizon. He told me he had asked you about it, and that you had convinced him it had no importance to us, so he hadn't pressed you about it. I agreed of course that it was your own affair, but ever since then I've wondered——'

Paula held her breath. Louise had been there at the dinner-table when Monique had dared their fate with the remark which at the time had had meaning only for Paula. So supposing Louise too had remembered it and was adding it up to suspicion as Gratien had done? But it seemed Louise had been checked only by embarrassment as she went on to repeat, 'I did wonder whether you had offended Gratien with your refusal to discuss it, and that could be why he has been so distant since?'

Paula admitted, 'I think he didn't like my refusing. But it really was past history, and not important any more.'

'And he should have accepted that,' Louise agreed, then sighed. 'Such a pity, if he has let such a triviality offend him. Not like him at all. One way or another, it wasn't a very big issue, was it? One can only suppose that he was disappointed that you didn't feel you could confide in him.'

'Disappointed?' Paula queried. There had been no disappointment to the cold reserve of Gratien's final question to her; only the contempt which he thought she had earned.

'Yes. Disappointed, hurt. After our getting to know you so well and growing as fond of you as we are,' explained Louise, attributing feelings to Gratien which, if he had ever experienced them, had them for her no longer, Paula felt wretchedly certain.

She and Louise went on to talk about Monique and Hans. Louise had also had a letter that morning from Madame Gautier, announcing her engagement to Fabian Touquet, and Paula said she had heard the same news from Monique.

'This Monsieur Touquet is rich, which will ease Hélène's problems a lot,' said Louise. 'She has always behaved as if the world owed her the life of luxury she couldn't afford. Maman helped her with Milon's and Monique's schooling, but I know she has wanted Monique to marry well, so one rather wonders what she thinks of Hans Brittel as a prospective *parti*, or whether it doesn't matter now, now that Hélène herself is going to be more than comfortably placed.'

'From her letter to Monique, I believe that's so,' said Paula. 'At any rate, she wrote quite kindly about Hans, telling Monique to take him home to meet her.' Paula felt her softening of Hélène Gautier's grudging complaisance was justified when Louise, pleased, said, 'That's good. Monique has been a changed girl since she met Hans. She has always been rather gauche and ungracious, and this time when she came to us, she seemed to be carrying a new black devil on her shoulder. It is only since Hans——' Louise broke off. 'Well, one must only hope he is serious about her, and from the time he wants to spend with her, it seems he is. So perhaps she and her mother may arrange to have a double wedding,' Louise concluded sunnily.

When they had parted for the night and Paula was back in her little suite she looked around it with affection. In the short time she had occupied it, she had grown used to it and attached to it, and meant not to denude it of her personal things until the last possible minute before she had to leave it. But among her own books there were still two which she had borrowed from Gratien, and it occurred to her that now, while he was out, would be a good time to return them to the shelves in his office.

She found them and went downstairs. Though knowing he was still out, from habit she knocked at his door before going in. She replaced the books and, as always when she came here, her glance went in search of the technical treatise where she had found Louise's sketch of herself. She had opened it once or twice since, and the sketch had still been there. When she opened the book now, for the last time, it would be there——

It wasn't. She riffled through the pages, held the book upside down by its covers, so that the leaves, opening fanwise, must release any loose sheet between them. Nothing fell out. And so—Gratien hadn't forgotten where he had put it! He had remembered, and since the last time she had been here he had taken it out, probably to destroy. And even if he had ever kept it out of some kindly feeling towards her, it was easy to guess the point at which he had had no further interest in it.

She wished now with all her heart that when Louise had complained in his hearing that it was lost, she had told them both she knew where it was. She could have done it lightly, pretending only to remind Gratien that he must have forgotten finding it. But now it was too late. Now she would never know the truth of whatever impulse had made him purloin it in the first place.

As she stood irresolutely for a moment, the book in her hands, there was a sound from the hall, the front door opening and shutting and then Gratien's voice.

Usually, when he dined at Aragon, he did not return until after midnight, and it was not yet eleven. There was someone with him too—Monique, as Paula knew from the answering voice. They must have arrived home at the same time and met outside. They continued to talk, while Paula debated whether to leave the office and join them or to wait until they had parted company; any meeting with Gratien was fraught with embarrassment for her nowadays.

She heard their footsteps cross the hall and Monique's 'Goodnight', as if Gratien were not going upstairs with her. But he would hardly come to his office at this hour; more likely he was going to the *salon* to pour himself a nightcap. That meant the coast was clear. Paula replaced the book she held, opened the office-door quietly—and came face to face with Gratien on the threshold.

'Oh——' She backed away from him and he came on in, closing the door behind him. 'I came to return the last books I borrowed from you,' she explained.

'And I've sent Monique to ask you, if you were still up, to come down and see me.'

'You—wanted me?'

'If you would come. Ah——' He turned to open the door to Monique, who began, 'She isn't there,' then stopped at sight of Paula. 'Oh, you've found her yourself.'

'Yes.'

'And so,' Monique hesitated, 'you don't want me?'

With a brief smile, 'Not at the moment,' Gratien said.

Monique still lingered. 'You wouldn't like me to explain? How? Why?'

'I think I can do it for you. Meanwhile——' the slight jerk of his head was significant, and Monique took the hint. She looked at Paula. 'Please listen to him,' she begged, then went out, closing the door behind her.

'Won't you sit down?'

There was only one chair, other than the one behind the desk. Paula sat, upright and tensed, while Gratien pulled his own forward to sit opposite to her, almost knee to knee.

'Paula, why didn't you tell me?' he asked very gently. 'All that I've heard from Monique tonight?'

'From Monique—since you both came in just now?'

'No. I took her out to dinner this evening, and we've talked.'

'Oh, I thought she was with Hans, and that you——'

'She didn't want anyone to know she had asked me to take her out. And I don't have to tell you what she wanted to confide to me, do I?'

Realising but incredulous, Paula said, 'About Barbizon? But she wouldn't have! All that was between her and me, and finished ... over.'

'Over? *Over*—while you let me believe it of you, in order to shield her? When, with a word, you could have stopped my judging you, despising you —and not for whatever it was that I believed you had done. I could have forgiven you that ... anything. But your refusal to trust me, your involvement of Monique, as I thought, in some shabby secret you wanted kept quiet—that did earn my contempt. When I taxed you, why didn't you tell me the truth?'

'I couldn't. It was Monique's secret and she was too frightened of her part in it coming out. Afraid lest her mother should hear it; afraid lest *you* should. But you mean she volunteered to tell you about it—wanted to?' Paula queried.

' "Had to" was her phrase.'

'But why? Why now, when it needn't ever have been told?'

Gratien's dark eyes narrowed in a smile. 'For a woman's reason, I gather. Because, she said, she was so happy herself, and hadn't the right to be, while sheltering behind you. Hans Brittel asked her to marry him this afternoon.'

'Oh. But she hasn't told him about Barbizon, has she?' queried Paula in alarm.

'She hadn't, and I advised her not to. It does a man good to put his girl on a pedestal, and the confession of an earlier unsavoury affair is no note on which to start a blissful engagement. Do you agree?'

'I think so. Though I'd hate to have something like that between me and——'

'Between you and——? Go on,' Gratien prompted.

'Between me and the—any man I loved.'

'That's better. You resort too much to phrases you don't finish, do you know? As for those two, there's no reason why it should be between them for ever. Monique says it never meant anything to her, and one day, when it's even farther behind her than it is now, she'll be able to tell it as a joke to Hans, and they'll both laugh together. And *she* can't be so innocent that she can imagine she is the first girl Hans ever kissed.'

Paula shuddered. 'But that Sallust! He was married and middle-aged.'

'Which lent him a certain glamour to Monique's eyes. Were you there, for instance, when she protested crossly to me that she preferred older men?'

'Yes.'

'In reference to me, that time.'

Paula stared. 'She told you that too? About her mother's pressure on her to make you interested in her?'

Gratien nodded. 'Once set upon unburdening

her soul, she unloaded everything.'

'Though why she thought she need,' mused Paula, 'just now, when she is leaving, and I am too, I don't understand.'

'She will be leaving. You will not.'

'But I shall, the day after tomorrow.'

'No. You and I have things to define to each other, Paula Raymond, and they may take time.'

Her heart skipped a beat. 'Things? Such as?'

'Feelings, attitudes, desires, hopes——' He reached to take her hand. 'For you, this "any man" you are going to love, or do love now—what kind of shape does he take? What do you want of him?'

'It's not fair to ask me that.' She had tried to stir her hand, but he held fast.

'It is fair. I have to know, wanting as I do, to be that man for you, the man you'll marry. Could I be—ever?'

'You? Me? Marry?' she echoed stupidly.

'It follows, doesn't it, when two free people are in love? And even when only one loves, is it so unfair for a man to tell his woman so? You haven't answered my question,' he reminded her.

'How can I, when it can't be true that you love me? There's never been anything between us. Nothing to show——'

'There could have been, if you had ever allowed it, or, while Crespigny was around, if I hadn't been eaten with jealousy of him. And then, when you had given your word that he meant nothing to you, this affair of your pact with Monique cropped up, and sheer pride and disllusionment wouldn't have let me tell you—or show you.'

'So that, if Monique hadn't ... talked, you would never have said anything of all this to me?' Paula questioned.

'I don't know, but I doubt if I could have let you go without giving you another chance to trust me. If you had still refused, I might not have been able to resist telling you that, whatever I felt for you, I meant to bury it deep and forget it as soon as you had gone. I'd have asked nothing of you in return.'

'You wouldn't have cared whether I loved you?'

'Cared? You ask me that? I'd have ached to know! But I wouldn't have asked.'

'Then you would never have known how long you've been in my mind and my heart and my first thought of every day,' she said in a whisper.

He flinched, then leaned to grip both her arms. 'Say that again,' he ordered. 'Say it again!'

She blinked back the starting, embarrassed tears. 'I shouldn't have to. You must know what it meant,' she told him.

'Ah!' He drew her to her feet and held her close. 'But how? When? A long time, you say? Tell me?'

She laughed softly. 'It began for me very early, but all the wrong way, as it had never done before——'

'There have been other beginnings for you? Other men?'

'One or two, but never in the way you ... happened to me. That was in a kind of thunderclap of physical attraction to you, your looks, your manner, your voice. But to love someone, I was sure I needed to know and like them first. So I could tell

179

myself that as long as I only fancied you in passing, I was safe.'

'You needed to feel safe from me? Why?'

'Because you employed me. Because I should be near you for only a few weeks. Because your life and mine were a whole world apart, different. And later, because of Solange. But by that time I knew I wasn't safe. Coming to love you for ... all that I do love you for, had happened the other way round, that was all.'

'You've thought I meant to marry Solange?'

'Everyone has seemed to hope it or assume so, including Solange herself.'

Gratien shook his head. 'Not she. Every time she comes here, she lays claim to all my attention. But for her I'm only a mirror to preen before, and a sounding-board of her potential appeal to men. For if she can believe I'm jealous or possessive of her, she takes that as a sign other men will be too, and she thrives on that. As primitive and uninhibited as a young savage, Solange Courtet. And though savages may make as merry playmates as puppies do, as wives in the long term they're apt to lack a lot that an adult man needs.'

'So she isn't in love with you?'

'As, whatever she may claim for effect, she very well knows.'

'Nor you with her?'

His smile was fond, indulgent. 'How you need to have it spelled out, *mignonne*! No, never near it in a thousand light years, even if you hadn't "happened", as you call it. Though for me it did happen in the way you seem to think is the right way round. We crossed swords that first day in Bordeaux, do you remember? You curled into a positive ball of aggressive hostility, and I thought "Here's a girl of character who'll be worth fighting", and the more we clashed later and made it up or compromised, the more I realised that this was what a lot of marriage was about—the give-and-take, cogs grating sometimes, but always running smoothly in the end. And realising that, I knew I mustn't ever let you go, because, after you, there would never be another like you for me. And it wasn't until later, after that first day, that all the rest happened and fitted in.'

'The rest?'

'Can't you guess? Loving—all this——' His hands touched her hair, cupped her face, travelled down her throat, outlined the swell of breast, the inward curve to narrow waist and the jut of slim hips beneath her thin dress. His hands dropped away and went to hold her close again. 'This,' he murmured thickly, 'I wanted—and *wanted* very soon after I had begun to enjoy the challenge of your mind, your character. Do you remember the day that reckless fool Milon risked killing you?'

'And you helped me up and held me for a minute longer than you need, I thought.'

'And almost too long for my self-control. If the time and the place had been different, I'd have swept you up and away then. Would that have been too soon for you?'

'I remember wishing that you had!'

'Yet you didn't understand what I was trying to say to you that night at Aragon after we had dropped the Cinderella fantasy?'

'I thought it was a kind of jealous recoil from Solange, and you said it was only your way of admiring how I looked.'

'It certainly wasn't recoil from Solange, and it was much, much more than admiration. It was homage to all that you were and are and mean to me— Paula, would you understand now, if I said it all again?'

To that her answer was in the shudder of ecstasy with which she surrendered her lips to the touch of his, at first lightly searching, then insisting that they share both their present rapture and the deep promise of future passion held in leash for too long.

They kissed and looked and touched, every sense alive to their delight of discovery. Now they were a little shy; now sure enough to tease, to joke, to laugh. Now tender; now urgently desirous. Now silent, but not withdrawn nor apart, their awareness of their new sweet rapport enough without need of words.

Time passed. Once Paula thought wonderingly, 'This isn't happening to me. It can't be true. I shall wake up——' But it was true, for here was Gratien, tall, virile and real, and asking the first prosaic question for ages.

'How did you happen to be in here, when I thought I should have to go and find you?' he asked.

'I told you—I came to return some books,' she said.

'Taking the opportunity to avoid me, because you knew I was out?'

'Perhaps,' she smiled provocatively.

'*Perhaps!*' he mocked. 'For that you deserve never to hear about the secret I kept from you here.'

'A secret?' She wondered whether she understood.

'In this.' He reached to hook a forefinger on to the spine of the volume she knew only too well, and drew it out. 'I knew you would never look into it, so the thing was quite safe.'

'And supposing I told you I had looked into it— several times?'

He stared. 'It would have no interest for you! It's all formulae and graphs!'

'I know. But I knocked it down by accident once, and something—the secret?—fell out.'

He laughed wryly. 'So you know? You've known?'

'I've opened the book and looked, every time I've been here when you weren't.'

'But didn't my having kept it say anything to you? Tell you?'

'No, it only puzzled me, and I couldn't ask. The only thing I've ever understood about it was its not being there any longer when I looked for it tonight before you came.'

'And what, my would-be wise one, did you understand about it then?' he teased.

'Why, that for whatever reason you had kept it earlier, you had destroyed it since; you despised me, and meant to let me go.'

'And what if I'd been tempted to destroy it, but couldn't, and found a better place for it—here?'

With one arm around her again, his other hand went to the inner breast pocket of his linen jacket and drew out Louise's sketch.

Paula took it from him. 'So you did want it, and want to keep it,' she breathed.

'Enough to steal it and admit nothing,' he agreed. He took it back from her. 'And here, next to my heart, it is going to stay until it wears away at its creases and falls apart. When Louise is famous, she shall paint you again, and we'll hang you with all the other de Tourcy ancestry at the head of the stairs!'

They laughed at that, and it was not until they agreed that perhaps it was time they parted for the night and went out into the hall, arms entwined, that Paula took in the significance of what he had said.

She looked about her, up at the great arch of the hall and the graceful sweep of the main staircase. 'You want to make me part of—of all this?' she marvelled. 'I shall be a de Tourcy like you, and *here* will be home; we shall be living here together?'

At that his smile was luminous, tender, a blessing. Then it crinkled into puckish humour.

'And what else do you think I meant when I said I intended to choose my own time for making Louise redundant as de Tourcy's châtelaine?' he wanted to know. And blew a finger-kiss as Paula laughed happily and ran away from him up the stairs.

Under its vaulted roof and between its cask-lined

walls the *chai* had been transformed into a dining-room, with two long tables flanking its length, joined by a cross 'top' table at one end.

The cloths, brought out from store year by year, were crimson; the lighting was by candles. The lack of space between each place-cover, and the crowding wine-bottles, dishes, plates, glasses and candlesticks on the tables made for much nudging and manoeuvring and the screech of chair-legs on the floor as people shifted position to give their neighbours more elbow-room or to claim more of the same for themselves.

The preliminary aperitif-drinking had been done in the *cuvier* next door. But now the serious business of the main meal was in full swing, to the accompanying music of shouted laughter and the chink and clatter of tableware being set about its work.

Wine danced into glasses and poured down throats with good reason. The harvest had been well above average; there were plenty of events, past and future, to be toasted; tomorrow was Sunday and tonight was all *couleur de rose*.

The top table was the prerogative of the white-collars and the squirearchy—the office and house staff, the vineyard manager, the cellarmaster, with Gratien and Louise in the places of honour, at centre-side of the table, facing down the aisle of the *chai*. Paula was on Gratien's right, Monique beyond the vineyard manager on Louise's left. Hans Brittel hadn't been invited; this was strictly a de Tourcy Château happening, a family affair.

Paula was living in a rosy glow of her own. Added

to last night's wonder that Gratien's love would make her a de Tourcy was an equally wondering gratitude that from now on she would be part of all the dedication and loyalty and camaraderie she was sharing now. Lovely people, all of them; earthy and cheerful, and jealous guardians of all that the château stood for in their lives, with long memories of past great vintages being quoted by the oldest of them to the youngest, and for all of them 'this season's' the traditional toast of the evening, however it matured.

Last night Monique, wide-eyed, curious to hear Paula's story and eager to tell her own, had gone to Paula's room after, she said, she had heard Gratien go to his.

Gratien, it seemed, had also done some confiding after Monique had made the confession to which conscience and bliss had driven her. Gratien had told her about Paula; that she was the only woman for him, and that even if Monique hadn't cleared her name, he had meant Paula should know it before she left.

Monique had reported, 'I said, "And what then? Where would just *telling* her get you?" And he said, "Nowhere", he supposed, but that he thought he'd get some savage satisfaction from telling you, without asking anything of you in return.'

At that Paula had laughed shakily. 'He little knew for how long he could have asked anything of me and it would have been there for him.'

'He explained about Solange too,' Monique had said. 'And to think of all my fret, for jealousy of her!'

'And you weren't the only one,' Paula had admitted. 'But just how and why did it come to you that you had to tell him the truth? I don't really understand why you thought you need?'

'Yes, well, it was after Hans had asked me to marry him. I made him take me to St Emilion——'

'I was in St Emilion yesterday too,' put in Paula.

'But not at the fountain? That's where we went. Hans said it was silly, to throw in pins when we had decided our own result. But I wanted to, and I did, and they crossed—they really did! And though Hans said it was only to do with the way the speed and swirl of the water varied, at least they told the truth—we *shall* get married within the year,' Monique had concluded a little breathlessly.

'But about Gratien and Barbizon?'

'Well, it was the pins doing their stuff for me, I think. I suddenly knew I had to clear you, or I wouldn't deserve Hans. I had to tell someone who would advise me whether I must tell Hans too. I was ashamed to tell Louise, and besides I thought Gratien would know best about telling Hans. But Gratien said No; that there was no point in spoiling Hans's image of me for the sake of something that had long been over and done with. But Gratien did want to know why I had sheltered behind you for all this time. He was pretty angry at first, until I told him why I was frightened, and he said he supposed that to me that was good reason enough.'

'But did you tell him that I had agreed with you that it was good reason enough?' asked Paula.

Monique had nodded. 'And he said, Maybe, but look how much time with you I had made him waste

—which rather got me on the raw. I said, If he had known, for as long as he claimed, that he was in love with you, why hadn't he got around to telling you so before all this suspicion of you cropped up? And as he didn't seem to have any answer to that, I'd say we parted quits!'

There had been Louise's reaction too. Evidently Gratien had gone into early conclave with her, for when, that morning, Paula had opened her door to, as she supposed, Rosalie with her *café complet*, it had been Louise who stood there with the tray; Louise, all smiles and eager questions and plans; Louise, saying over and over that she had never guessed, but that she had sometimes thought how lovely it would be if—— If they hadn't to lose Paula at the end of the season; if Gratien would marry someone *like* Paula; if, at least, Paula would come back to them next season. If ... if ... if. And now the ifs had turned into facts, and Paula wouldn't be leaving at all!

After that it hadn't been long before Emilie and Rosalie and Pierre had heard the news, and by now, when Gratien was saying he thought it was time to call the toast to the vintage, it was pretty certain that everyone present had heard it too.

Filled glass in hand, he was on his feet. The clatter stilled. 'To the vintage!' he proposed, and with an answering roar, the whole company was on its feet.

'And to all the vintagers!' he called, whereupon everybody drank willingly to themselves.

'And——' with one arm round Paula's waist—— 'to the bride I'll be making mistress of de Tourcy long before next vintage—drink!'

They drank and catcalled, and then, by tradition, the oldest vintager present called the toast to Gratien—*Monsieur le Vigneron*, and Gratien acknowledged it with thanks. The noise subsided a little, then at the far end of the *chai* someone said something which was greeted with a guffaw.

Heads wagged; ears were cocked. 'What was that? What was said?' people wanted to know. It was repeated from neighbour to neighbour; passed from mouth to mouth, the laughter it evoked growing louder and louder, rolling and washing like a gathering wave until it finally broke on the top table.

'What——?' asked Gratien, and a dozen shouting voices told him.

'He—was it Damien Suryat or his wife Francoise?—no matter, it was one of them—said "*Eh bien*, all the world knows that it's a wise man who marries his cook!"' the chorus yelled, reporting the wisecrack as if for sparkle, it had all other witticisms left at the post.

But whether or not Gratien thought so, he took it up. He called back to the Suryats—'A wise man, you say, *mes amis*? Well, wise or not, this one is marrying the loveliest cook in the world!' and taking Paula into his arms he kissed her full upon the lips before them all.

The roof-timbers of the *chai* creaked their protest at the uproar, and the glasses were filled again.

Send for free catalog

Most of these old favorites have not
been reissued since first publication.
So if you read them then, you'll enjoy
them again; if they're new to you,
you'll have the pleasure of discovering
a new series of compelling romances
from past years.

Collection Editions are available only
from Harlequin Reader Service. They
are not sold in stores.

Clip and mail this special coupon. We
will send you a catalog listing all the
Collection Editions titles and authors.

Harlequin Reader Service
MPO Box 707,
Niagara Falls, N.Y. 14302

In Canada:
Stratford, Ontario
N5A 6W4

Please send me, without obligation, your free Collection
Editions catalog containing 100 vintage Harlequin
romance novels.

NAME _____
(please print)

ADDRESS _____

CITY _____

STATE/PROV. _____ ZIP/POSTAL CODE _____

Offer expires December 31, 1977.

ROM 2066

Send coupon today for
FREE
Harlequin Presents
Catalog

We'll send you by return mail a complete listing
of all the wonderful Harlequin Presents novels
still in stock.

Here's your chance to catch up on all the
delightful reading you may have missed
because the books are no longer available at
your favorite booksellers.

Fill in this handy order form and mail it today.